I0619787

CONTENTS

CHAPTER 1

Morelville, Ohio

Mel and Dana pulled into their driveway in Morelville, Ohio, just as the sun began sinking below the horizon. The windows of their house glowed in the orange-tinted light radiating from the sky as dusk approached.

Mel could hear the excited barks of Dana's Boston Terrier, Boo, from inside the car.

"Sounds like someone missed their mom," she said with a grin to her wife, Dana, who sat in the passenger seat.

"More like she missed her treats," Dana retorted playfully, unbuckling her seatbelt. They had just returned from what was supposed to have been a long weekend getaway at their cabin in Tennessee, and despite being tired from the long drive, both women were eager to be reunited with their family.

As they stepped out of the car, the front door flew open, and Hannah emerged with her three-year-old son Jef clinging to her leg. "Aunt Mel! Aunt Dana!" Jef shouted, wiggling free from his mother's grasp and running toward the two women with his arms wide open.

"Hey there, buddy!" Mel scooped him up into her arms, squeezing him tightly. Dana kneeled down, allowing Boo to jump into her embrace, her tail wagging furiously.

"Everything went okay while we were gone?" Mel asked Hannah, still holding Jef.

"Smooth sailing here," Hannah replied with a smile. "Not so much for you, though. Are you okay?" Hannah asked Mel.

Mel grimaced. "Word travels fast. I'm okay. Let's just say I've had enough of Tennessee for a while, though."

"I bet. Let's get you two inside and settled." Hannah ushered everyone back into the house.

***

The next morning, Mel walked down the main street of Zanesville, Ohio, toward the courthouse, feeling that familiar comfort of small-town life. The aroma of fresh baked goods wafted from the local bakery, and she greeted business owners opening for the day by name as she passed them by. Despite the idyllic scene, Mel knew that her role as Sheriff was crucial in maintaining law and order for the county seat and the rest of the county.

"Morning, Sheriff!" called out Mr. Thompson, the owner of Thompson's Hardware Store, his voice warm and friendly.

"Morning, Mr. Thompson," Mel replied with a nod, continuing down the street. It was a tight-knit community where everyone seemed to know everyone else, and Mel felt a strong sense of duty to protect them all.

As she rounded the corner near the bakery, Mel spotted one of her deputies, Pete, leaning against his cruiser, sipping a cup of coffee.

"Morning, Pete," she greeted him, her boots tapping authoritatively on the pavement. "Anything to report?"

"Quiet day so far, Sheriff," he answered, tipping his hat to her. "Nothing but the usual small-town stuff."

"Good," Mel said, her thoughts drifting back to her family waiting at home. She knew her job demanded much of her time and attention, but lately, she had wanted to spend more time with Dana, Jef, and her niece and nephew, Beth and Cole, away from the demands of law enforcement.

"Enjoy your morning, Pete," she said, patting him on the shoulder before continuing her walk through town. As she passed the familiar storefronts, Mel couldn't help but wonder again, as she had even before her ordeal in Tennessee, if it might be time to pass the Sheriff's badge to someone else, allowing her to focus on what mattered most to her—her family.

Just as Mel was about to enter the courthouse to confer with the deputy DA, Andrea Anderson, her phone buzzed in her pocket. It was a text from her lead detective, Shane Harding.

"Urgent meeting in my office, ASAP," the message read.

She called him.

"I'm at the courthouse. What's up?"

"I know you're just getting back, Sheriff, but this Cutlass case with your brother-in-law's old car is bizarre," he began without preamble. "We still don't have an ID on the victim. The coroner says blunt force trauma killed him. No murder weapon in or around where the car was when Lance picked it up...er, attempted to pick it up, and few usable prints anywhere that aren't from Lance or--"

"Or my erstwhile nephew, Cole?"

"Yeah," Shane admitted. "What's the story here, anyway? I figured you might have some insight into this since it's family."

"Give me a few minutes to get back to my vehicle and get back over to the department. This is a story better told in person."

Her reason for wanting to see Andrea was more personal than professional and would have to wait.

*＊＊

With Shane for the first time since she'd returned, she rebuffed his attempts to ask her about what went down in Tennessee, instead focusing on the new case at hand. "It's crazy," she told him. "Lance got that car from his dad when he was sixteen. He sent it out for some auto body and interior work and then for storage when he was twenty because he was moving out of state to work with his dad. He and his mother had divorced, and he had moved to Arizona."

"When Lance returned a couple of years later, the car was gone, auctioned off a few months before as part of the contents of a barn that went up for auction when the property owner - the guy who had been working on the car - died. Lance had kept up the insurance on it and the registrations and still had legal rights to the car."

"He thought he got a lead several years ago when someone tried to get a salvage title for it, but it never panned out. He couldn't find the guy. Then, it turned up right here in the county, a few months back. He's been jumping through hoops to prove it's his and get it back ever since someone who knows him and the story of his car spotted it in front of a shade tree type auto repair shop and called him."

Shane whistled softly. "That's one hell of a story. And now, after all these years, the car turns up with a body in the trunk? This isn't going to be a simple investigation."

"Nothing ever is around here," Mel muttered, her thoughts reeling. "Anyway, I guess we better get to work. We need to figure out who this poor soul is and how he ended up in the trunk of Lance's car."

"Agreed," Shane said, determination etched on his face. "I'll get the forensics reports all gathered up and when Mason gets in, we'll both start digging into this."

"Keep me updated," Mel ordered, her voice firm but tinged with a hint of worry. Despite her internal conflict about her career, she knew that solving this mysterious case was essential - not only for the sake of the victim, but also for her brother-in-law and their family.

"Of course, Sheriff," Shane assured her. With a quick nod, he left the office he shared with Mel's other detective, Janet Mason, and headed down the hall, already pulling out his phone to call the forensic unit in Columbus who had scoured the car.

Mel watched him go, feeling the weight of the investigation settle on her shoulders. Her thoughts drifted momentarily to her wife and all the rest of her family, as she wished for more time with them. But that would have to wait.

She pushed away her personal concerns and focused on the task at hand. Pulling out her own phone as she walked toward her office, she started making calls to gather any possible information about the body found in her brother-in-law's car.

For the rest of the morning, Mel and her assistant Holly spent their time contacting other law enforcement agencies in the area, asking if they had any missing persons cases that might match the description of the unidentified victim.

As the hours went on, Mel found herself immersed in the case. The mystery surrounding the body in the trunk continued to grow; there were no immediate leads or connections to explain how it had ended up there. As frustrating as it was, Mel felt a familiar spark of determination light within her–the drive to solve the seemingly unsolvable.

When the day slowly turned into early evening, Holly went home, but Mel remained in her office, poring over every detail and piece of evidence they had gathered so far. She knew that somewhere within the tangled web of information, there had to be an answer. And she wouldn't rest until she found it.

As the darkness of the early spring night settled in, the on-duty desk sergeant buzzed her office phone and called her to come up front if she could. Mel decided she needed the break anyway and stepped out of her office. She knew she needed a clear head to think about the case objectively. Walking down the hallway, she caught sight of Dana waiting for her near the entrance of the station.

"Hey, you. Long day, huh?" Dana asked, concern clear in her eyes. She handed her wife a bag with supper in it Hannah had cooked and packaged up for her as she'd done many times before.

"Longer than I expected for the first day back. But I'm glad you're here," Mel replied, managing a weary smile. She held up the bag. "Thanks for this."

"I was betting you hadn't eaten."

"Holly brought me back a turkey club for lunch."

"Which was probably about seven hours ago, Mel." They moved away from the front desk, into the hallway, and Dana softened her tone. "Have you thought about what we talked before things went sideways down there? About stepping down as Sheriff?"

Mel sighed and leaned against the wall, her mind racing with conflicting thoughts. "I have, but it's not that simple. You know how much I love this job and the responsibility that comes with it. But I can't deny that it takes a toll on me and our family."

"You love being a cop. You don't love being the sheriff. Not what the job has become, anyway."

At Mel's answering nod, Dana went on, "Listen, I'm not trying to force you into anything, but after everything that's happened–especially that hostage situation during our getaway–maybe it's time to consider other options. You've done so much for this community, Mel. No one would blame you if you wanted to step back and enjoy life a bit more."

Mel closed her eyes, letting Dana's words sink in. She couldn't help but think about Jef's smiling face when she returned home and Boo's excited barking. The thought of spending more time with them and Dana, and her dad, whom she knew was ailing whether or not he admitted it, was undeniably appealing. Yet, the weight of her duties as Sheriff still hung heavily on her shoulders.

"Let's talk about this more when I get home tonight, okay?" Mel suggested, trying to find a compromise for now. "I promise, I'll give it serious thought, Dana. But right now, I need to focus on this case. I can't let the victim and their family down."

"Alright," Dana relented, understanding the importance of Mel's commitment to her work. "Just promise me you won't stay all night, okay? You've been through a lot. We're all here for you, Mel."

With a nod, Mel watched as Dana turned to leave before stepping back into her office. She knew she had some significant decisions to make about her future, but first she had a case to solve.

"Shane, what's the latest on the body-in-the-trunk case?" Mel asked as her lead detective entered her office.

"Still unidentified, Mel," Shane replied, looking grim. "We're working with the state crime lab to see if they can pull anything from the remains. The car's registration and insurance paperwork are old and all in your brother-in-law's name, but we found a few personal items that may help us get to a name."

"Good," Mel said, rubbing her temples. Despite her internal conflicts, she knew she couldn't let them interfere with her job. "Keep me updated on the progress. This guy has family somewhere and they deserve some answers."

"Of course, Sheriff," Shane nodded, understanding her dedication. "I'll let you know as soon as we get any new information."

"Thanks, Shane." Mel sighed as he left her office, her thoughts once again drifting to her conversation with Dana and the future she had to consider. She stared out the window at the streets of Zanesville, thinking about how much her life revolved around maintaining order in this community. And paperwork. Lots of paperwork.

Chapter 2

As Mel strode up the steps of the county courthouse in Zanesville, she tugged at the collar of her uniform, feeling the weight of the badge on her chest as she mentally prepared for her meeting with Deputy DA Andrea Anderson. The body-in-the-trunk case had been gnawing at her, but it wasn't the only thing on her mind. Her potential resignation as the sheriff loomed large, the decision heavy on her shoulders.

"Mel!" a voice called out just before she reached the doors, and she turned to see County Commissioner Todd Bell closing the distance between them, his brow furrowed with concern. "You got a minute?"

"Depends," Mel replied. "What's this about?"

"Word's getting around about that body in the trunk of that old car," Todd said, wiping a bead of sweat from his forehead. "People are panicking. Rumors are spreading fast."

"Rumors?" Mel asked, crossing her arms over her chest.

"Wild theories, mostly. You know how it is in a small town like this," Todd said, shaking his head. "I've even heard talk about a serial killer or a satanic cult."

"Are you serious?" Mel exclaimed, rolling her eyes. "We both know better than to believe that nonsense."

"Of course, but it's not about what we know; it's about what the community thinks. Fear breeds more fear. We need to get ahead of this, Mel."

"Look, I'm doing everything I can to solve this case, Todd," Mel snapped, her patience wearing thin.

"But are you doing everything you can to keep the peace, Sheriff?" Todd shot back, his tone growing sharp. "Or are you too busy contemplating your resignation?"

The tension between Mel and Todd was palpable, their long history of professional rivalry and conflicting personalities clear in their heated exchange.

"Maybe if you spent more time supporting me instead of second-guessing my every move, I wouldn't be thinking about resigning," Mel retorted, her voice rising.

"Support you?" Todd scoffed. "I'm the one who convinced you to run for sheriff in the first place, remember? But what do I know?"

"Right now, all I need from you is to trust that I've got this handled," Mel said through gritted teeth. "Now, if you'll excuse me, I have a meeting with Andrea."

She brushed past him, her frustration simmering just beneath the surface. As she entered the courthouse, Mel couldn't help but wonder if she was making the right decision, both regarding the case and to her future as sheriff. The pressure was mounting, and it seemed like everyone had an opinion–but ultimately, the choice was hers alone to make.

"Hey, Andrea," Mel greeted as she entered the Deputy DA's office, trying to shake off her annoyance with Todd. "Ready to talk about the body-in-the-trunk case?"

"Of course," Andrea replied, her professional demeanor a welcome contrast to Todd's antagonism. "What updates do you have for me?"

Mel quickly filled Andrea in on the latest developments, including the discovery of a small amount of trace evidence and the identification of at least one potential suspect, though Mel felt in her gut the guy who had possession of the car last would be ruled out. He had no prior brushes with law enforcement. Not even a parking ticket. As they discussed the intricacies of the case, Mel couldn't help but feel grateful for Andrea's level-headed approach.

"Any thoughts on where we should focus our efforts?" Mel asked, seeking input from both Andrea and Todd, who had followed her into the office despite their earlier disagreement.

"Based on what you've told us, I think we need to look more closely at the victim's personal life," Andrea suggested. "There might be connections there that we haven't considered. Do we have a positive ID, yet?"

"The body was fresh enough the Columbus Crime Lab could lift fingerprints from him along with the trace they found under his nails. They're backlogged, but we should have something any time now."

"I'll see if I can get a line on it. I've got some pull with the brass over there," Todd chimed in begrudgingly. "We can't overlook any leads, even if they seem insignificant at first."

"Alright," Mel nodded, appreciating their insights. "I'll give you a couple of hours, then make sure my team follows up with the lab."

Wanting a more private conversation with Andrea, Mel closed the door behind Todd as he left. She knew that beyond their professional relationship, Andrea was also a supportive friend–one who understood the unique challenges she faced as a lesbian in their line of work even though Andrea remained closeted.

"Thanks for having my back," Mel said softly, leaning against the now-closed door.

"Of course," Andrea replied with a reassuring smile. "You know I'm always here for you, Mel."

"Trust me, I appreciate it more than you know," Mel sighed, feeling some of the weight lifting from her shoulders. "Especially with everything going on right now."

"Let's just focus on solving this case," Andrea suggested. "Everything else will fall into place."

Mel nodded in agreement, grateful for her friend's unwavering support. And with that mutual understanding, they dove back into their discussion.

As they continued their conversation, Mel couldn't help but feel the internal conflict tugging at her. The pressure of being the sheriff, solving cases like the body-in-the-trunk mystery, and maintaining a public image weighed heavily on her. She couldn't shake the nagging thoughts about how much she missed spending time with her wife, Dana, and their getaway cabin in the Smoky Mountains. The job had taken a toll on her, both physically and emotionally.

"Hey," Andrea said, catching Mel's far-off gaze. "Are you okay?"

Mel hesitated, not wanting to burden her friend with her personal struggles. But Andrea seemed genuinely concerned, and it was becoming harder for Mel to keep everything bottled up.

"Actually..." Mel began, her voice cracking slightly. "I've been seriously considering stepping down as sheriff."

Andrea studied her friend's face, searching for any hints of doubt or regret. She knew how much the job meant to Mel, but she could also see the strain it was causing her.

"Have you talked to Dana about this?" Andrea asked gently.

"Yeah. We've discussed it quite a bit," Mel admitted. "She's been incredibly supportive, as always. But I just... I don't know if I can do this anymore."

"Mel, if that's what you truly want, then you have my full support," Andrea assured her. "Your happiness and well-being are more important than any job title."

"Thank you," Mel whispered, feeling a sense of relief wash over her. "It means a lot to hear you say that."

"Of course, you know Todd is going to try to convince you to stay, and to keep running for reelection," Andrea warned, a wry smile playing on her lips.

"Doesn't he always?" Mel countered, smirking despite the gravity of the situation. "But I think it's time I put myself and my family first."

"Whatever you decide, I'll be here for you," Andrea promised, offering a comforting hand on Mel's shoulder. "Now, let's get back to work and crack this case wide open. Who knows–maybe it'll help you make your decision."

***

After another a long day at work, Mel paid a visit to her best friend Barb Wysocki to discuss her thoughts further. As she pulled into the driveway of Barb's home, she felt a warm sense of familiarity and comfort wash over her–just what she needed after the turmoil of emotions she had been experiencing lately.

"Mel, it's so good to see you!" Barb exclaimed, hugging her tightly as soon as she stepped through the door. "I've been worried about you."

"Thanks, Barb," Mel replied, returning the embrace. "It's been quite a couple of weeks."

"Come on in, and let's talk," Barb gestured towards the living room, where they settled down on the sofa. Mel wasted no time in sharing her internal struggles, seeking the input of her trusted confidante.

"Mel, you know I'll always have your back, no matter what," Barb said sincerely, placing a hand on Mel's knee. "I think you do a lot of good things for this county, but if stepping down as sheriff is what's best for you, Dana, and your family, then that's what you should do."

"Thank you, Barb," Mel responded gratefully. "Your support means a lot to me."

"Of course, you know Janet and I will be here for you too," Barb added, referring to her wife, one of Mel's detectives. "We're all in this together."

"Speaking of which, we should get everyone together for dinner this Friday night," Mel suggested, her spirits lifting at the thought of spending time with her closest friends. "What do you think?"

"Sounds perfect," Barb agreed enthusiastically. "Let's invite Andrea too, if you think she'll come. The more, the merrier!"

***

When Friday evening arrived, the atmosphere at the Italian restaurant they chose in Reynoldsburg, an hour outside Zanesville, buzzed with laughter and conversation as Mel, Dana, Barb, Janet, Andrea, and Andrea's guest gathered around a large table near the window. The glow of the street lamp outside Scali cast a golden hue over their faces, lending a sense of intimacy and camaraderie to the occasion.

"Everyone, I'd like you to meet my friend, Renee," Andrea introduced her guest with a smile, before sitting down beside her. There was something about the way she looked at Renee that hinted at a deeper connection between them, adding a touch of intrigue to the evening.

"Nice to meet you, Renee," Mel greeted the newcomer warmly, extending a hand across the table. "We're glad you could join us tonight."

"Thanks for having me," Renee replied, shaking Mel's hand firmly. "Andrea told me a little about all of you on the way here."

"Only good things, I hope," Barb joked, raising an eyebrow playfully as everyone chuckled.

"Of course," Andrea assured her, a teasing glint in her own eyes.

"Renee, how did you and Andrea meet?" Dana asked, sipping her wine and turning the conversation back toward their guest.

"Ah, that's a story," Renee said, glancing at Andrea with a grin. "We met in law school. We were both studying late one night at the library, and as fate would have it, we reached for the same book at the same time."

"Like something out of a movie," Andrea chimed in, laughing.

"Except without the romantic music playing in the background," Renee added, causing everyone else to chuckle.

"Did you two hit it off right away?" Janet inquired, genuinely curious about the connection between the two women.

"More or less," Andrea replied, looking thoughtful. "We had our differences – I was more focused on criminal law, while Renee leaned toward corporate law – but we found common ground in our shared passion for justice and helping others."

"Speaking of which," Renee interjected, "Andrea's been a great mentor to me over the years. She's really helped me navigate some tricky situations in my career. I'm grateful to have her as a friend."

"Likewise," Andrea agreed, again smiling warmly at Renee.

As the night unfolded, the group engaged in lighthearted banter, sharing stories and memories. The women opened up to each other even more, discussing topics ranging from work to family and everything in between. Mel felt a sense of gratitude wash over her for the opportunity to relax and enjoy the company of her friends. The weight of her decision seemed to lift, if only for a few hours.

"Here's to good friends and new beginnings," Barb proposed, raising her glass in a toast as the evening drew to a close.

"New beginnings," the others echoed, clinking their glasses together, a symbol of unity and friendship.

Mel couldn't help but smile as she took in the faces of her closest allies. She knew that no matter what decision she made about her role as sheriff, these people would be there for her–and that was a comforting thought. Mel felt a renewed sense of hope in the possibilities that lay ahead, not just for herself, but for Andrea and Renee as well.

CHAPTER 3

F aye Crane stood at the kitchen window, staring out at the budding trees in the distance. She twisted the dish towel in her hands, the damp fabric releasing a faint scent of lemon. "I just don't understand why we have to go on this trip the week before Easter, Chloe," she said, her voice tight with concern.

Chloe Rossi leaned against the counter, her arms crossed over her chest, a determined glint in her eye. "Faye, it's going to be fine. We need this vacation, and I've found the perfect place near Pigeon Forge."

"Perfect or not, it's still the week before Easter," Faye insisted, shaking her head. "What if something happens while we're away? What about the church services and the preparations? And Jesse..." Her voice trailed off as she thought about her ailing husband who refused to see a doctor.

"Jesse will be with us," Chloe reminded her, unfolding her arms and placing a comforting hand on Faye's shoulder. "He could use the break too, and Mel can handle things back here if she decides not to go. Besides, I've already booked the lodge. It's got more than enough space for all of us—even your grandkids, and Mel and Dana, if they decide to stay with the family instead of over at their cabin."

Faye glanced over at Chloe, her expression softening slightly as she considered the other woman's words. She knew Chloe was right; they all needed a break, especially after everything that had happened recently. But the timing...it weighed heavily on her mind.

"Chloe, I know you mean well, but this is important to me. I don't want to miss our family traditions."

"Neither do I, Faye." Chloe held up her phone, a picture of the lodge displayed on the screen. "Just look at this place! It's got a huge living area, a game room, and even an indoor pool. The kids will have a blast, and we can leave Saturday morning. We'd be home late Saturday afternoon. You can make it to the sunrise service, make Easter dinner - whatever you want."

Faye hesitated, her gaze lingering on the image of the lodge. It did look inviting, and she couldn't deny the excitement that bubbled up inside her at the thought of spending time with her family in such a beautiful place. But her concerns remained, stubbornly refusing to be dismissed.

"Chloe, I..." Faye started, but Chloe cut her off.

"Trust me, Faye. This trip will be good for all of us," she said, her voice firm but gentle. "We'll be creating lots of new memories together. Now, let's get packing. Tennessee awaits!"

With one last glance out the window, Faye reluctantly nodded. She could see the determination in Chloe's eyes, and deep down, part of her longed for the escape too. "Alright, Chloe. Let's do this."

***

Mel stood in the kitchen doorway, listening to the conversation between Chloe and Faye. She couldn't shake the unease that settled in her gut at the thought of returning to Tennessee so soon after the hostage incident. And with the body in the trunk case still looming over her head, the timing felt off. But the excitement in Chloe's voice was contagious, and Mel couldn't help but feel drawn to the idea of a family vacation.

"Hey, Mel," Dana called from behind her, breaking her out of her thoughts. "What do you think? Are we going?"

Mel hesitated, weighing her responsibilities against the opportunity for a real, much-needed break. "I don't know, Dana. The timing... it's just not great."

Dana approached her wife, placing a comforting hand on her shoulder. "I know you're worried about the case, Mel, but you need this. We all do. Besides, it's a chance for you to talk to your parents about the future."

Mel sighed, knowing Dana was right. Her father Jesse had been struggling to maintain their small herd of cattle, his health clearly declining. It was time to have a serious discussion about the farm's future and her own role in it. "You're right," she admitted. "Maybe this trip is the perfect opportunity to have those conversations."

"Exactly," Dana said, giving Mel a reassuring squeeze. "And who knows? Maybe some time away will give you a fresh perspective on the case, too."

With a determined nod, Mel decided. "Alright. Let's go to Tennessee. I'll set things up with Shane and Janet before we leave, so they can handle any new developments in the case while I'm gone, and I'll help dad round up some help to make sure the herd is moved from pasture to pasture while we're gone and to keep an eye on things."

"Great!" Dana beamed, pulling Mel in for a quick hug. "Now let's get home and get packing. The Smoky Mountains are calling our names...er, again."

Mel couldn't help but feel a mix of apprehension and excitement. She knew there were important conversations ahead, and the weight of her responsibilities still hung heavy on her shoulders. But maybe, just maybe, this vacation would offer the clarity she needed to face the challenges that lay before her.

***

Mel barely had time to settle into her office chair on Monday morning when Detective Shane Harding burst through the door, a triumphant grin plastered on his face. "Mel, we got an ID on the body in the trunk!" he announced, holding up a file.

"Already?" Mel asked, surprised by the swift progress. She had been mentally preparing herself for a long, drawn-out investigation. "What have you got?"

"Not crime lab. They're still backed up. His name is Greg Foster, age 34," Shane replied, handing over the file. "Lived in Licking County, near Hebron. He was reported missing about ten days ago to the Hebron PD by his sister after she hadn't heard from him for a couple of days."

Mel rocked in her chair, as she nodded. "That would be about right. Any idea how he ended up in the trunk?" Mel inquired, scanning the information in the file.

"Not yet, but Janet and I are working on it," Shane assured her. "We're going to pay a visit to his sister today to gather more information, see if they can shed any light on why someone would want him dead."

"Good. Keep me updated, Shane," Mel instructed. As she looked at the photo of the deceased man taken in life, she couldn't help but feel a pang of sympathy for the family. Even though she was desperate for this vacation, she knew she couldn't leave without ensuring the case was in capable hands.

"Of course, Sheriff. We'll handle everything while you're gone," Shane said with confidence. He dropped his tone. "You deserve a real break, Mel. Don't worry; we've got your back."

"Thanks, Shane. I appreciate that." Mel offered him a grateful smile before diving into the details of Greg Foster's life, determined to uncover the truth before leaving for Tennessee.

As Mel pored over the reports, she couldn't shake the nagging feeling that this case was far from straightforward. It was as if the deeper she dug, the more questions arose. Who was Greg Foster, really? And who would go to such extreme lengths to end his life?

After a long day at the office, Mel returned home to find her family excitedly discussing their upcoming trip. Hannah had decided to close her bakery so she and Jef could go. With Chloe's consent, she'd even invited her girlfriend Morgan and her toddler.

She couldn't help but smile at the enthusiasm for the trip in her own household, even as her thoughts were occupied by the case that refused to release its grip on her.

"Hey, everything okay?" Dana asked, noticing the troubled expression on Mel's face.

"Shane and Janet have made some progress on the case, but there's still so much we don't know," Mel admitted, her brow furrowing in concern. "I'm trying not to let it get to me, but I can't help feeling like I'm leaving them with an unfinished puzzle."

"Mel, you've prepared them well, and they're capable detectives," Dana reassured her, wrapping an arm around her shoulders. "You need this time away to recharge and reconnect with your family. You can't solve every case overnight, and sometimes stepping back for a moment can give you the clarity you need to see things from a new angle."

"Maybe you're right," Mel conceded, leaning into Dana's embrace. As she looked around at her family, their excitement for the trip infectious, she knew she owed it to all of them—and herself—to make the most of their time together in Tennessee.

With a deep breath, Mel pushed her lingering concerns about the case to the back of her mind and turned her focus to the trip preparations. She started making mental lists of what needed to be done before they left—packing clothes, stocking up on groceries, and ensuring their vehicles were ready for the long drive.

"Alright, let's get moving! We have a lot to do!" Mel announced, injecting energy into her voice as she clapped her hands together. Her family responded with enthusiasm, and soon everyone was bustling around the house, gathering their belongings and checking off items on their individual to-do lists.

Amid the chaos, Mel felt grateful for the distraction from her work. As she packed her own suitcase, she allowed herself to daydream about the long walks through the woods that she and Dana would take, and the precious moments she'd share with her nieces and nephews. She even looked forward to the conversations she planned to have with her parents about their plans for the farm.

The next day, Mel found herself in the barn with her father, Jesse. The smell of hay inside and the soft sounds of their small herd of cattle milling about in the pasture outside filled the air. She leaned against a wooden post, watching her father as he went about his chores.

"Hey, Dad," she began, hesitating slightly before continuing, "I've been thinking about something lately, and I'd like to talk to you and Mom about it during our trip."

Jesse paused, wiping the sweat from his brow as he turned to face his daughter. "What's on your mind, Mel?"

His voice had a little more roughness than his usual gruff tone, but he looked at her with interest, so she pressed on. "Maybe...maybe it's time for me to step down as Sheriff," she admitted, her voice barely above a whisper. "I want to spend more time with my family, and help more around the farm, especially with how things have been going lately."

Jesse's eyes softened as he took in her words. He knew his daughter had always shouldered more than her fair share of responsibility, both professionally and within their family. "It's a big decision, Mel. But we'll be there to support you, no matter what you choose. We certainly won't turn down the help. Capable help. The boy is learning, but he isn't you." He offered her a shrug and crooked grin, high praise from him.

"Thanks, Dad," Mel said, feeling some of the weightlifting from her shoulders. "I just thought it was time we started talking about the future of the farm and what's best for all of us."

"We can do that," Jesse agreed, nodding. "Let's set aside some time during the trip for a good, long talk."

His agreement surprised Mel. He wasn't one who easily asked for help or conceded he might need it.

"Don't go saying anything to your mother, just yet, though. You know how she'll fret about it."

She knew.

***

As their travel day drew closer, suitcases and bags piled up near the front door. The atmosphere in the house was a mix of anticipation and excitement. Mel could feel the energy building as everyone eagerly awaited their departure the next morning.

"Hey, just wanted to let you know, I've got everything prepared for the animals while we're gone, including Boo, and Kris's dog," Jesse announced as he entered Mel and Dana's kitchen where the two women were double-checking their packing list.

"Thanks, Dad. I'm sure that's a huge load off your mind," Mel replied gratefully. It was a load off her own mind. Knowing that having someone taking care of all their pets and livestock gave her one less thing to worry about during their vacation.

"Are you all set here?" Faye asked, as she and Chloe came inside too, and Faye joined them in their kitchen. "I think we've packed everything inside the farmhouse and Chloe's store."

"Looks like we packed our whole house, too," Mel said as she glanced around at the various bags and suitcases. "We'll load everything up in the morning, and then we're off to Tennessee."

"Can't wait," Chloe chimed in from the doorway, a broad grin on her face. "It's going to be so much fun!"

Mel smiled at her mother-in-law's enthusiasm and felt a renewed determination to make the most of their time together, leaving her work behind for a few precious days. With one last glance around the room, she knew that despite the hectic preparations and lingering thoughts about the case, this trip would be an opportunity they all needed–a chance to reconnect and create lasting memories as a family.

"Alright everyone, get yourselves home and try to get some rest," Mel announced, as the excitement in the room settled. "Tomorrow, we begin our adventure."

Dana gave Boo a hug and handed him off to Faye for the trip to the family that would care for him for the next week. "Not this trip, buddy," she whispered. "This cabin doesn't allow dogs. You'll always be allowed at ours."

Later that evening, after everyone had gone home, Mel and Dana found themselves alone in their living room. The silence weighed heavily on Mel's mind as she thought about the unsolved case and how it would be left in the hands of her team while they were away.

"Hey," Dana said softly, taking a seat next to Mel on the couch. "You've been quiet since everyone left. What's going on?"

Mel sighed, running a hand through her short hair. "I can't help but think about the case, Dana. I'm worried about leaving it behind, even just for a week."

"Mel, you deserve this break. You need to recharge and spend some time with your family, especially with everything that's been going on lately," Dana replied, placing a comforting hand on her wife's shoulder.

"I know," Mel admitted, leaning into Dana's touch. "It's just hard to shake that feeling of responsibility. But you're right, we all need this vacation together."

"Shane and Janet are capable, and they'll keep you updated if anything significant happens," Dana reassured her. "Your deputies will handle everything else, and Holly will handle everything that moves through your office. "Now, let's try to enjoy the time we have before the trip, okay?"

Mel nodded, forcing a smile. "Okay."

***

The day of their departure finally arrived, and a sense of anticipation buzzed through the air as the family gathered outside the side-by-side homes of Mel and Kris. Multiple vehicles were packed with luggage, food, and supplies for the week-long vacation. Mel stood beside Dana, exchanging last-minute instructions with Shane over the phone.

"Remember to keep me updated on the case, but don't hesitate to make decisions if you need to. I trust you and Janet," Mel said firmly.

"Understood, Sheriff," Shane replied. "You just enjoy your vacation. We've got everything under control here."

"Thanks, Shane," Mel said before hanging up and turning her attention back to her family.

"Is everyone ready?" she called out, looking at the excited faces of her loved ones. There were nods and murmurs of agreement as they climbed into their respective vehicles.

"Alright then," Mel announced, feeling a hint of excitement herself. "Let's hit the road."

The convoy of cars rolled out onto the country road, heading for their Tennessee getaway. As they left Morelville behind, Mel allowed herself momentarily to forget about the pressure of her job and focus on the adventure that lay ahead–an adventure that might just change the course of her life forever.

CHAPTER 4

As late afternoon descended on their convoy, the Crane and Rossi families finally reached their destination. The atmosphere was abuzz with energy and enthusiasm as they laughed and chatted about all the fun things that awaited them in Pigeon Forge along the way.

"Look at this place!" Cole exclaimed, his eyes widening as they pulled up to the cabin. Nestled among the towering trees, the wooden structure looked like a cozy retreat from the hustle and bustle of everyday life.

"Wow," breathed Beth, equally impressed. "I can't believe we get to stay here for an entire week!"

"Let's take a good look around," Mel said to the kids as Chloe put in the key code and lead the group inside. The interior was warm and inviting, with large windows that bathed the rooms in golden sunlight.

"Check out the heated pool!" Dana said, pointing to the enclosed sunroom off the back of the main level. Crystal clear water shimmered beneath the surface, inviting them to take a dip despite the slight chill of mid-March in the mountains outside.

"Thank goodness for that," Marco commented, rubbing his hands together. "Who would've thought it'd still be so cold in the Smokies this time of year?"

"Hey, it wouldn't be a proper family vacation without some unexpected surprises," Chloe joked, earning chuckles from the others.

"Speaking of surprises, have you seen everything Pigeon Forge offers?" Mel asked the kids, unfolding a brightly colored brochure. "There's go-karts, mini-golf, zip lines, alpine roller coasters, and even a trampoline park!"

"Really?" Cole's eyes lit up at the mention of go-karts. "We've got to try some of that out while we're here."

"Absolutely," agreed Beth, her enthusiasm bubbling over. "This is going to be the best vacation ever."

"Agreed," said Faye, smiling warmly at her granddaughter. "Now, let's get settled in and start exploring with dinner in town first. We can cook tomorrow."

"Sounds like a plan," Mel replied, already envisioning the memories they'd create together as a family.

Later that evening, when the tots and teens were finally asleep, Lance and Jesse found themselves on the spacious deck overlooking the wooded landscape. The cool mountain air was refreshing as they leaned against the railing, beers in hand.

Lance brought up their fishing plans for the next day. "I can't wait to hit Douglas Lake tomorrow," he said, his enthusiasm clear. "But are you sure it's not too cold this time of year?"

"Ah, don't worry about it," Jesse reassured his son-in-law. "I checked the forecast, and besides, I've got us some top-notch gear to keep us warm. We're going to catch us some fish out there."

"Sounds perfect," Lance replied, clinking his beer bottle against Jesse's. "I'm glad we can do this. It's been too long since we last went fishing."

"Couldn't agree more," Jesse said with a nod. "It was worth the long ride down here, don't you think?"

"Absolutely," Lance affirmed, taking a sip of his beer.

Inside, Marco who usually loved to fish excitedly discussed the haunted house convention in Gatlinburg with Dana and Mel instead. His eyes sparkled with anticipation as he spoke of the event and the rumored potential sale of a local haunted house.

"Can you imagine owning our very own haunt, right here in Tennessee?" Marco asked, the excitement in his voice palpable.

Dana and Mel exchanged concerned looks. While Dana shared her father's love for running a haunted house, she didn't want it to become a permanent fixture near their getaway retreat. The annual three-week fundraiser they used to do for the Pittsburgh Jaycees back where she grew up, and the Fall Festival haunt they helped with now in Morelville were more than enough for her.

"Uh, Dad," Dana hesitated, "as much as I love helping with the temporary haunted house back home, I'm not sure I'd want one that we'd have to run as a business, full time and all the headaches that come with that."

"Right," Mel chimed in, "this place is our escape from the hustle and bustle of everyday life. Having to run a business, a haunted house business with all the regulations and liability would change all of that."

Marco seemed thoughtful for a moment before nodding in understanding. "You have a point, girls. But I still can't wait to see what they have going on at the convention. Who knows? Maybe we'll come across some new ideas for our annual haunt back in Morelville."

"Can't argue with that," Dana agreed, smiling softly. "Just keep in mind, it's only one weekend a year to raise money for the community center." She knew her father's enthusiasm for haunted houses wasn't going anywhere, but she was grateful he respected their concerns about keeping their Tennessee retreat a sanctuary. As the family settled in for the night, they eagerly anticipated the adventures awaiting them in the days to come.

The next morning, Dana checked in with her friend and boss, Yvonne, who lived in Tennessee. Grabbing her phone, she sent a text to Yvonne.

Dana: "Hey, Yvonne! We made it to the cabin last night. Any chance you're not on the road and free for lunch today? Mel and I would love to catch up."

Yvonne: "Hi Dana. Sure thing, I'm free around noon. How about we meet at that little café by the river in Gatlinburg where we had coffee once before? Looking forward to seeing you both!"

Dana: "Sounds perfect! See you then," Dana replied, excited at the opportunity to spend some time with her friend.

As the family members gathered in the living room after breakfast, they began discussing their individual plans for the day.

"Jesse and I are heading out to Douglas Lake for some fishing," Lance announced with enthusiasm as prepared to leave.

"Good luck, boys!" Kris called out after her father and husband as they grabbed their gear and headed for the door.

"Thanks! We'll try to catch something big enough for dinner," Lance grinned.

"Marco and I are going to explore the haunted house convention in Gatlinburg," Chloe chimed in, linking arms with her husband.

"Have fun and don't buy anything too spooky," Mel warned playfully.

"Promise," Marco replied. His mischievous grin gave him away.

Cole said, "Mom, can we go too? I want to see all that stuff."

Surprised at her oldest, Kris asked. "I thought you wanted to go down on the parkway and hit the arcades and go cart tracks?"

"We have all week for that, right Beth?"

"I really want to do that," Beth told her brother.

"Please come with me," he pleaded with her.

Beth gave in. "I'll go and protect you, big brother. I know you're afraid of the dark."

"Am not..."

"Mel and I have a lunch meeting with my friend Yvonne, but other than that, we're just planning on enjoying the sights and sounds of Pigeon Forge," Dana interrupted their bickering to share.

"Can't wait to see what trouble we get into," Mel joked, giving Dana a quick kiss on the cheek.

With everyone's plans set, the family members went their separate ways.

Later that morning day, Mel and Dana walked into the small café where their lunch meeting with Yvonne was scheduled. The warm aroma of fresh coffee and baked goods filled the air as they spotted Yvonne waving from a corner booth.

"Hey, you two!" Yvonne greeted them enthusiastically as they approached. "It's been too long..... what, two or three weeks?"

"Yvonne, it's great to see you in a more normal situation," Mel replied with a genuine smile, while Dana offered her friend a hug.

Yvonne looked Mel up and down. "I hate to say it, but you still look a little drawn out after...well, you know, being held hostage and all. How are you holding up?"

"Let's just say I'm surprised to see myself back down here so soon," Mel said.

"Let's catch up over some good food, shall we?" Dana suggested as they settled in.

As they perused the menu and placed their orders, the conversation flowed easily among the trio. They chatted about family, work, and life with laughter punctuating their stories.

"Mel, I heard a rumor that you're considering stepping down as Sheriff," Yvonne mentioned casually as she sipped her iced tea. "Is there any truth to that?"

Mel shot Dana a look before responding. "Yes, I've been giving it some thought. I've decided not to seek re-election when my term is up."

"Really? What brought on this decision?" Yvonne asked, her curiosity piqued. "I hope it wasn't what happened here. That was such a crazy fluke."

"Truth be told, I've been feeling a bit worn out for a while now," Mel admitted, taking a deep breath. "I love serving my community, but the stress has taken its toll over the years, especially since becoming the sheriff. The paperwork. The politics. Plus, I want to spend more time with my family."

"Those are valid reasons, Mel," Yvonne nodded in understanding. "Have you thought about what you'd like to do next?"

"Teaching law enforcement has crossed my mind," Mel shared, her eyes lighting up at the idea. "I think I could make a difference by sharing my knowledge and experience with others."

"That sounds like a fantastic plan," Yvonne encouraged. "You have so much to offer, and I think you'd be an amazing teacher."

"Thank you, Yvonne," Mel replied, feeling a sense of relief and validation wash over her. "I appreciate your support."

"Of course," Yvonne smiled warmly. "And if there's anything I can do to help, don't hesitate to reach out."

"Thanks, I'll keep that in mind," Mel said, feeling grateful for Yvonne's offer. "I'm still weighing my options, so it's good to know I have people in my corner."

"Always," Yvonne affirmed. "You've got a genuine gift for connecting with people and helping them see their potential. Whatever you choose to do, I know you'll excel at it."

"Changing careers can be daunting, especially at our age," Dana chimed in, her hand resting on Mel's. "But I believe in you, babe. You've always had a knack for adapting and overcoming challenges."

"Thank you," Mel responded, squeezing Dana's hand gently. She knew she was fortunate to have such a supportive partner by her side.

"Besides, it's never too late to start something new," Yvonne added. "People are reinventing themselves all the time. The key is to follow your passion and stay true to yourself."

"You're absolutely right," Mel agreed, taking Yvonne's words to heart. "I need to focus on what truly matters to me—my family and making a difference in others' lives. Whether that's as a sheriff or a teacher, I'll find my way."

"Exactly," Yvonne said with a reassuring smile. "Just remember, life is full of surprises. Embrace them, learn from them, and trust the journey."

The conversation flowed naturally as the three women continued discussing Mel's plans and reminisced about their own experiences and career paths.

As the lunch meeting drew to a close, Mel felt an odd mix of emotions—uncertainty and excitement mingling inside her. She looked at Dana and Yvonne, grateful for their support. "Thank you both," she said sincerely. "I can't express how much I appreciate your advice and encouragement."

"Anytime, Mel," Yvonne replied warmly. "I'm here for you, no matter what you decide."

With that, they gathered their belongings and headed out of the restaurant, their laughter and conversation filling the air as they walked back toward their respective vehicles.

CHAPTER 5

The harsh fluorescent lights of the convention center buzzed overhead, casting a stark glow on the rows of booths and displays. Dana and Mel entered through the main doors, their eyes scanning the sea of people gathered for the haunted house convention. They spotted Dana's parents and Mel's mom near the far end of the room.

"Over here!" Marco called out, waving them over with a broad grin. His excitement was palpable, even from a distance.

Dana exchanged a glance with her wife, amused by her father's enthusiasm. Mel shrugged and smiled as they made their way through the crowd. "He's like a kid in a candy store," she said, chuckling.

"Can't say I blame him," Dana replied, taking in the array of creepy animatronics and elaborate set designs surrounding them.

As they reached Dana's parents, Marco pulled them both into a tight hug. "You two have got to see this guy's work–it's amazing!" He pointed at a booth nearby, where a tall, thin man with hawkish features demonstrated his creations. "His name's Devon, and he's an electronics genius!"

Mel raised an eyebrow, intrigued. "Animatronics?"

"Yep! He builds these incredible figures for haunted houses." Marco's eyes shone with admiration as he gestured towards the ghoulish creatures that adorned Devon's display. "It's not just the craftsmanship; it's the technology behind it all. He's got sensors that detect movement, synchronized lighting... you name it."

Dana watched as the man finished speaking with another attendee and turned to face them. Devon's sharp gaze took them in, assessing them in a split second. She felt a shiver run down her spine. "Well, let's go talk to him then. He seems free now."

"Great idea." Marco eagerly led the way, with Mel and Dana following close behind.

"Devon," Marco said, extending his hand. "My name's Marco Rossi, and this is my wife Chloe, my daughter Dana, and her wife, Mel."

"Nice to meet you all," Devon replied, his voice smooth and confident as he shook their hands. "What brings you to my corner of the convention?"

"Your animatronics caught my eye," Marco admitted. "The level of detail and realism is astonishing."

"Thank you." Devon gestured to a life-sized zombie that lunged forward suddenly, causing Dana to jump back, startled. Marco laughed, clearly impressed.

"See what I mean?" Marco grinned at Mel and Dana. "You really feel like they're alive... or undead, in this case."

Dana couldn't help but agree. She watched as Devon continued showing the various features of his creations, noting the pride in his eyes as he explained the intricate inner workings of each one.

"Have you always been into animatronics?" Mel asked him, genuinely curious.

"Ever since I was a kid," Devon answered, a wistful smile playing on his lips. "I've always loved the challenge of bringing something to life through technology. There's something about watching people react to my creations that never gets old."

"Who needs to hunt for real ghosts when you have these, right?" Dana joked, earning a chuckle from Devon.

"Exactly," he agreed, turning to face his next potential customer.

As they walked away, Marco continued to gush about Devon's talents, already dreaming up ways to incorporate such animatronics into his own work for the community haunted house.

"Let's just hope we don't end up taking one of those things home," Mel muttered under her breath, a playful smirk on her face.

"Hey, you never know," Dana replied, grinning. "It might just give our cabin that extra touch of spookiness."

As they were all about to explore the rest of the convention, Devon hurried over to them, a sense of urgency in his voice. "Hey, I almost forgot. If you're interested, there's a behind-the-scenes tour happening tomorrow at a haunted house just down the parkway. They've got a lot of my creations there and I'll be setting up several more. It's limited though, so I'd recommend signing up soon if you want to join."

"Behind-the-scenes?" Marco's eyes lit up at the prospect. "That sounds amazing! What do you think, Dana? Mel?"

Dana glanced at Mel, who seemed to weigh the idea in her mind. "Could be interesting," she agreed cautiously. "Alright, let's do it."

"Great!" Devon beamed at them. "Just head over to Wesley Collins's booth to sign up. He's the owner of the haunted house and the one organizing the tour."

"Thanks, Devon. We'll definitely check that out," said Marco, already heading in the direction he pointed.

As they approached Wesley's booth, they found the older man engaged in conversation with a group of enthusiasts. His enthusiasm was infectious, and he spoke animatedly about his experiences in the haunted house industry.

"Ah, hello there!" Wesley greeted them warmly as they approached, extending a hand for each of them to shake. "I'm Wesley Collins. Are you here to sign up for the behind-the-scenes tour?"

"Devon told us about it," Mel explained, returning his firm handshake. "Sounded intriguing, so we thought we'd give it a shot."

"Fantastic! You won't be disappointed," Wesley assured them, a glint of excitement in his eyes. "There will be a traditional in the dark walk through for those who are interested, followed by a lights on, behind-the-scenes tour, and then a talk and a display by Devon. Sound good?"

"Sounds great," Marco said.

"How many of you will do the traditional in the dark tour?" Wesley asked as he consulted a schedule on a clipboard.

They all looked around at each other. Everyone but Faye committed to it, but Chloe gave her a nudge and a wink. "I'll hold your hand. Marco won't know I exist anyway."

When Faye committed, Marco told Wesley, "It looks like all of us, plus you better add in two teenagers too. He tipped his head toward Beth and Cole as the teens joined them."

"Well, since you're all joining that part of the tour, I'd like to offer you a special experience - actors for the traditional in the dark walk-through with the next tour group after yours. What do you say?"

Marco, Cole, and Dana exchanged glances, considering the offer. The prospect of seeing a commercial haunted house from the behind-the-scenes perspective in both the light and the dark was undeniably alluring.

"Sounds like an offer we can't refuse," Dana said, a determined gleam in her eyes. She gave her dad a playful nudge as she said, "Count us in."

"Excellent!" Wesley clapped his hands together, delighted. "I promise you, this will be an experience you won't forget."

***

"Alright, everyone," Wesley announced as they prepared to enter the darkened haunted house. "Remember to stay together and enjoy the experience."

As the group crossed the threshold into the eerie darkness, Slater, a pretty young woman who had caught Cole's eye earlier, sidled up to him with a mischievous grin. Her flirtatious nature was apparent, and Cole couldn't help but feel both flattered and intrigued.

"Hey, I'm Slater," she said, her voice barely above a whisper, as if sharing a secret. "You're Cole, right?"

"Uh, yeah," Cole replied, trying to keep his cool despite feeling his heart race. He wasn't used to such direct attention, especially from someone like Slater.

"Looks like we're in for some fun today," she continued, her eyes twinkling with excitement. "I've always been a fan of haunted houses. You too?"

"Definitely," Cole agreed, his confidence growing. "They're like an adrenaline rush, you know? Never knowing what's around the corner."

"Exactly," Slater nodded, her hand brushing against his arm. "And it's even better when you have someone to share it with."

Cole took a deep breath, feeling the electricity between them. He knew he should focus on the haunted house tour and the behind-the-scenes opportunity, but Slater's presence made it nearly impossible to concentrate on anything else.

"I agree," he finally managed. "It's...uh, nice to have someone here who gets it."

"Let's stick together then," Slater suggested, her smile widening. "We can watch each other's backs and make this night one to remember."

"Deal," Cole agreed, his pulse quickening as they ventured further into the shadows, side by side.

As the walk through in the dark ended, the group emerged back into the dimly lit entry area, their hearts still pounding from the adrenaline rush. Cole tried to catch his breath while stealing glances at Slater beside him, her flushed cheeks and bright eyes making her even more attractive.

"Wow," Dana exclaimed, "that was intense! I can't wait for the behind-the-scenes tour!"

"Me neither," Faye chimed in, her voice shaking slightly. "I hope they reveal some of their tricks. Some of those scares were so realistic."

"Alright, everyone," a staff member announced, "we'll be starting the behind-the-scenes tour shortly. Feel free to take a break, and we'll meet back here in ten minutes."

As the group dispersed to grab drinks or use the restroom, more people started to join them, having skipped the traditional walk through in the dark. Some appeared eager, while others seemed apprehensive about what awaited them on a fully lit, behind-the-scenes tour.

"Hey, isn't that Blake from back home?" Dana whispered to Mel, pointing towards a familiar face in the crowd. Beside him stood a woman with long, dark hair and an air of mystery about her.

"Looks like it," Dana confirmed. "What are the odds?"

"Small world," Kris muttered, exchanging glances with Beth.

Blake spotted the group from Morelville as well and raised a hand in greeting, clearly surprised to see them there. "Hey, Mel. Dana. Everyone. Fancy running into you all here." He approached them, Elena following close behind.

"Hey, Blake," Mel replied, her tone guarded. She never quite trusted him, but she had to admit that his presence added an interesting twist to the evening.

"This is my date, Elena," Blake said, introducing the woman. "They're all from Muskingum county too," he told her.

"Nice to meet you all," Elena said, her voice soft and polite. "Blake's been filling me in on Morelville," she added with a smile. "It sounds like quite an interesting place."

"Interesting is one way to put it," Mel said dryly, her eyes never leaving Blake.

"Hey, we're all here for a good time, right?" Blake countered, trying to diffuse the tension. "Haunted houses, behind-the-scenes tours... Sounds like a perfect night out!"

"Let's hope so," Mel replied, her gaze lingering on him for a moment before turning back to the rest of the group. She had a nagging feeling that something was off, but she pushed it aside, focusing instead on the upcoming behind-the-scenes tour.

As the group chatted and mingled, Mel couldn't help but notice a man about Slater's age, who stood off to the side, arms crossed over his chest, glaring intently at Cole and Slater. His jealousy was palpable, and Mel made a mental note to keep an eye on him throughout the evening.

"Alright everyone interested in doing the scare for the next traditional walk through, gather around!" Wesley Collins called out, drawing the attention of the tour group. "We're going to assign roles for that before we do the behind-the-scenes tour so you can get a feel for your area. This is your chance to get into character and experience the haunted house from the other side!"

The group clustered together, anticipation buzzing in the air. Wesley produced a clipboard with a list of roles for the participants. As he read through the options, he paused when he spotted Cole.

"Ah, young Mr. Crane," Wesley said with a grin, looking directly at Cole. "I think we have just the role for you. How about playing a Mike Myers-esque character? You know, the classic slasher movie villain?"

Cole hesitated for a moment, glancing at Slater, who was grinning at him encouragingly. The idea of being part of the action excited him, even though it was slightly unnerving. "Sure, I'll give it a shot," he said, trying to sound enthusiastic.

"Perfect!" Wesley clapped his hands together. "Everyone else, look at the list and choose your roles. We'll gather again in a few minutes to go over instructions and prep for the walk-through."

As the group huddled around to pick their roles, Mel couldn't shake the feeling that something was brewing beneath the surface, like a storm waiting to break. She glanced over at the man who'd been watching Cole and Slater once more. She could see him seething as Cole and Slater laughed together. Her instincts told her to stay alert and pay close attention to everyone's actions. After all, she had learned the hard way that appearances could deceive, and danger often lurked in the shadows.

As the group reconvened in anticipation of Devon's animatronics demonstration, Mel couldn't help but feel her senses sharpen. The air seemed charged with electricity as everyone gathered around the tall, thin, hawkish-looking man in his 40s.

"Alright, folks," Devon began, clearly excited to showcase his creations. "Before we dive into the behind-the-scenes tour and the next traditional walk-through, I'd like to give you a little taste of what you'll be experiencing. Animatronics are an essential part of any haunted house, and I've spent years perfecting my designs."

His enthusiasm was contagious, and even Mel leaned in, eager to see what he had in store for them. She glanced at her family members, noting that they too were captivated by Devon's passion for his craft.

"Allow me to introduce you to some of my latest creations," Devon continued, gesturing towards a collection of life-sized figures shrouded in darkness. "These animatronics have been designed to strike fear into the hearts of anyone brave enough to enter our haunted house. Are you ready?"

The group collectively held their breath, eyes fixed on the dark shapes ahead. Devon stepped forward and flipped a switch, bringing the figures to life. Suddenly, the room was filled with an eerie symphony of creaking joints, sinister laughter, and blood-curdling screams.

Mel watched as the animatronic monsters lurched and swayed with unnerving realism. Despite being aware that these creatures were nothing more than metal and silicone, she couldn't deny the chill that ran down her spine.

"Amazing work, Devon!" Marco exclaimed, his eyes wide with admiration. The rest of the group murmured their agreement, each person visibly impressed by the display.

"Thank you, thank you," Devon replied, basking in the praise. "But this is just a small sample of what awaits you on the tour." He flipped a switch on his control panel. "Now, if everyone's ready, let's move on to—"

Suddenly, the room was plunged into darkness. The animatronics ground to a halt, their mechanical noises replaced by an eerie silence. In the pitch black, Mel instinctively reached for her family members, her heart pounding in her chest.

A shrill scream pierced the darkness, chilling her to the bone.

Several seconds ticked by, then the lights flickered back on, casting a harsh glow across the room. Mel's eyes widened in horror as she took in the scene before her.

Slater lay motionless on the floor, her lifeless eyes staring blankly at the ceiling. A pool of blood was quickly forming around her body, and Cole stood over her, his hands gripping what appeared to be the murder weapon—the Michael Myers knife Wesley had given him.

"Wha–I didn't... I swear!" Cole stammered, his face pale with shock.

"Everyone, stay calm," Mel commanded, her authoritative voice cutting through the hysteria that threatened to engulf the group. She approached Cole slowly, her mind racing as she tried to process the situation. "Cole, put the knife down."

"I didn't do this, Aunt Mel," he insisted, his voice trembling. "It was dark, and then—"

"Put the knife down, now," Mel repeated firmly, her gaze locked onto his. Cole hesitated for a moment, then carefully placed the weapon on the ground and stepped away from it.

"Is she really...?" Chloe whispered, unable to take her eyes off Slater's lifeless form.

"Dead," Mel confirmed grimly. "We need to call the police."

As sirens wailed in the distance, Mel couldn't ignore the nagging feeling that Cole was being set up. He was no killer, but the evidence against him was damning. Her gut told her that there was more to this case than met the eye, and she was determined to find out the truth.

When the police arrived, Mel intercepted them, flashing her sheriff's badge from Muskingum County. "I'm Sheriff Mel Crane, and I'm in charge of this crime scene until one of your lieutenants or your chief gets here," she announced. "The primary suspect right now appears to be my nephew, and I request that he be remanded into my protective custody during the investigation."

"Are you sure you can be impartial, Sheriff?" one officer asked skeptically.

"Absolutely," Mel replied, her voice unwavering. "But I know this family, and I know this boy. I won't rest until the truth is uncovered."

As Cole was handcuffed and led away from the rest of the group, Mel felt a heavy weight settle on her shoulders. The stakes were high, and she knew that the road ahead would be difficult.

"Listen up, everyone," Mel addressed her family, her voice laced with determination. "We're going to help the local police investigate this murder. I don't trust them to handle it alone, and we can't just stand by while Cole is in custody."

The group exchanged glances, uncertainty clouding their faces. They knew Mel was right, but the prospect of diving into a murder investigation was daunting.

"Mel, are you sure we can do this?" Kris asked, her concern clear. "We're not all experienced investigators like you, Dana, and her dad."

"Experience or not, we have a unique perspective on the case, and we know Cole better than anyone else. We need to use that to our advantage," Mel replied.

"Alright," Marco agreed, his eyes lighting up with determination. "Let's do this. For Cole."

"Right," Faye chimed in, her grip tightening on Mel's arm. "We'll support you, Mel. We'll find out who really killed Slater and clear Cole's name."

"Thank you," Mel said, her heart swelling with gratitude for her family's unwavering support. "Now let's get to work."

CHAPTER 6

M el stood at the edge of the crime scene, her eyes scanning the area for any overlooked clues. As she turned her gaze to the crowd that had gathered, she spotted Brad Marsh—the man who'd been staring holes through Slater and Cole. She took a deep breath and strode over to him.

"Brad," Mel said, her voice firm but not unkind. "I need to ask you some questions about Slater."

"I'm waiting to talk to the local PD investigators, Sheriff," Brad replied, his eyes darting away from hers for a moment before he focused back on her face. "I don't have to talk to you."

"Humor me for just a minute," Mel told him. "They're going to be a while." She knew that from repeated experience with them.

As they spoke, Mel couldn't help but observe Brad's body language and demeanor. She noticed the way his fingers clenched and unclenched, betraying an underlying tension. His posture was rigid, almost as if he were trying to make himself appear larger or more intimidating. And his eyes—they held a hint of jealousy, possessiveness even, that made Mel's gut twist in unease.

"Did you see Slater at all today before... this happened?" Mel asked, gesturing toward the crime scene that lay behind her.

"No," Brad said, his jaw tightening. "We used to date, but I haven't seen her since we broke up. She didn't want anything to do with me after that."

Mel nodded, noting the bitterness that laced his words. She knew relationships could bring out the best or worst in people, and it seemed Slater's breakup with Brad might have done the latter.

"What brought you here today?"

He looked away as he replied, "I used to work here when I was a teenager. I heard about the animatronics Wesley added and about the demo today. Thought I'd take a look."

"Alright," Mel said, making a mental note of Brad's reactions. "I have a few more questions about your relationship with Slater," Mel continued. "Were there any issues or conflicts between the two of you that might have caused tension?"

"Conflicts?" Brad hesitated, his eyes narrowing slightly. "I mean, we fought sometimes, like any couple. But nothing serious."

"Can you give me an example of what you might have argued about? Were there ever any incidents where things got out of hand?"

"Out of hand?" He scoffed. "No, not really. We had our disagreements, sure, but it never got violent or anything. It's just... she was always flirting with other people, even when we were together. I didn't like that, but I never laid a hand on her."

Mel listened attentively to Brad's responses, searching for inconsistencies or red flags. She knew jealousy could be a dangerous emotion, and if Brad felt threatened by Slater's flirtatious nature, it might have given him a motive.

"Did you ever confront Slater about her behavior? How did she react when you expressed your concerns?"

"Of course I did," Brad said, his voice growing louder. "But she just laughed it off, told me I was being too possessive. She didn't care how I felt."

Mel observed the anger in his voice, the way his fists clenched at his side as he spoke about Slater. It was clear that their relationship hadn't ended amicably, and the unresolved feelings between them may have festered.

"Thank you for sharing that with me, Brad," Mel said calmly. "It's important that we gather as much information as possible. If you think of anything else, please talk to me about it."

As she walked away from Brad, Mel couldn't help but feel a growing suspicion towards him. His jealousy and possessiveness, coupled with the lingering resentment towards Slater, made him a person of interest in her mind. But she needed more evidence before drawing any conclusions. The investigation was far from over, and Mel knew she had to consider every angle before narrowing down her list of suspects.

Just as Mel finished her conversation with Brad, she noticed Blake Wagner approaching her. Blake was a gunsmith from Morelville, and his smarmy demeanor had always raised red flags for Mel. Despite his questionable reputation, he seemed to have something important to share.

"Hey, Sheriff," Blake said, conveying his distrust of law enforcement through his tone. "I'm not really one to confide in cops, but I've got to hand it to you—you've always been fair. I think I might know something about what happened here."

Mel raised an eyebrow, curious about what information he had to offer. Despite her personal reservations about him, she needed to be open to any possible leads, no matter where they came from.

Mel responded cautiously, trying to keep her skepticism in check. "I appreciate your willingness to come to me. What do you know?"

As they began their conversation, Mel steeled herself against any bias or preconceived notions about Blake and their past run-ins. If she was going to solve this case, it was crucial that she remain objective and impartial in her pursuit of the truth.

"So, just before the blackout, Elena started acting weird," Blake began, lowering his voice as if worried about being overheard. "She stopped talking to me and then disappeared. Said she needed to use the bathroom. I can't say for sure, but I think she might have been up to something."

Mel's interest peaked at the mention of Elena, who was already on her radar given her association with Blake. Keeping her expression neutral, she probed further. "Did you see her do anything, Blake? Can you be more specific?"

Blake hesitated, looking around before continuing. "She didn't come back, at least not until after the lights were on and we all saw the dead woman on the floor. She came back by me, but she wouldn't talk to me. She seemed pretty nervous, glancing around like she didn't want anyone to see her. Then, I just heard her tell one of the local cops she was with me the whole time."

"What did you tell them?"

"They haven't interviewed me yet, and when they do, I'm not telling them anything. I'm not getting in the middle of it.

Mel weighed the credibility of Blake's account, knowing that his history of distrust toward law enforcement could influence his version of events. However, dismissing his information outright would be unprofessional and could hinder her investigation.

"Thank you for sharing that with me, Blake," Mel said, making a mental note of his statement. "I'll look into it, but please keep this conversation between us for now. If Elena is involved, we don't want her knowing that we're onto her."

"Fine by me," Blake agreed, a hint of satisfaction playing across his face.

As Blake walked away, Mel couldn't help but consider the implications of his claims. If true, Elena could very well be connected to the case—perhaps even the culprit. But first, she needed to corroborate his story, gather more evidence, and possibly find a motive.

"Hey, Dana," Mel called out to her wife, who had been observing the scene at a distance. When Dana joined her, she confided, "I need you to talk to Elena Reyes. See if you can get her to open up about what she was doing during the blackout."

"Got it," Dana replied with a nod, knowing that her background in customs investigations and more recently in insurance fraud investigations would be useful in assessing Elena's behavior and credibility.

Dana approached Elena, who stood alone near the front ticket booth, looking uneasy and trying to avoid eye contact with the officers milling about. She noticed the woman's hands fidgeting with her purse strap, betraying her nervousness.

"Hi there, Elena," Dana began, offering a warm smile to put her at ease. "I'm Dana Rossi-Crane, Mel Crane's wife. I wanted to talk to you for a moment, if that's alright."

Elena glanced around before responding, her voice barely above a whisper. "Sure, I guess."

"Great. So, I heard you were here when the blackout occurred, but I had glanced around and noticed Blake watching the demonstration," Dana said, diving straight into the topic. "I didn't see you. Can you tell me what you were doing during that time?"

Elena hesitated, biting her lip as she gathered her thoughts. "Well, I went to the restroom just before the lights went out. When they did, I got scared, so I stayed there for a while until someone came looking for me."

"Who found you?" Dana asked, her mind working to piece together the timeline of events.

"Uh, it was Blake," Elena admitted, the color rising in her cheeks. "He got me back out here."

"Did you notice or hear anything unusual during the blackout? Anything that might help us understand what happened?" Dana pressed further, watching Elena's reactions closely.

"I... I don't know. It was dark, and I was panicking. I didn't really pay attention to anything else," Elena replied, her gaze darting around the room as she spoke. Her cell phone buzzed in her purse, and she glanced down at it.

"Do you want to get that?"

"It's nothing," Elena said. "Just a friend, worried about me, is all."

"Worried because of the murder?"

"No," Elena admitted. "Worried about Blake. It sounds like you're from his town. Do you know him?"

"I know more of him, than anything," Dana said.

"We've talked online quite a bit. He seemed so nice. Today is the first time we met. He's actually pretty creepy. Stalkerish, even. I live half the year in Zanesville, but I've been down here since we started talking a few weeks ago. Now I don't want to go back home up there."

Elena pulled her phone out and held it out to Dana. "Here. Look. It's my 'help me' text to my friend.

Dana looked. The text was time stamped several minutes before the lights went out.

"Dana handed the phone back. "Thank you for sharing that with me," she said, making a mental note of the woman's responses and body language. "If you remember anything else, please let Mel or me know."

"Sure, I will," Elena agreed, her voice trembling slightly. "Please don't say anything to Blake."

"You have my word."

As Dana walked back to Mel, she couldn't shake the feeling that something about Elena's story didn't quite add up. She knew they would need more information and evidence to determine whether the woman was truly involved in the case or simply someone looking for love in all the wrong places.

Dana found Mel again and waited for her to finish speaking to another woman who had been part of the joining tour group before she approached her.

"Did you talk to Elena?" Mel asked quietly, not wanting to draw any unwanted attention from the onlookers who were still lingering around the crime scene.

"Yes," Dana replied, keeping her voice low as well. "She claims she was in the restroom when the blackout occurred, and she sent a 'help me' text to a friend before the lights went out. She wasn't getting good vibes from Blake."

"Interesting," Mel mused. "Did she mention anything about her prior relationship with Blake?"

"Only that they've been talking online and today was the first time meeting each other in person. She said he's been acting creepy and somewhat stalkerish," Dana answered, recalling Elena's words and demeanor.

"Sounds like him, as we well know," Mel said, casting a sidelong glance at Blake, who was now standing off to the side, arms crossed and wearing a scowl. "Keep an eye on both of them. We need to dig deeper into their backgrounds and connections. There might be something there that ties one or both of them to this case."

"Will do," Dana agreed.

Just as Mel was about to speak again, a woman barged into the scene, her face red with anger and her voice loud enough for everyone present to hear. "You have no right to keep my son here! Release him immediately!" she demanded, pointing at Brad who was still standing nearby.

"Ma'am, you need to calm down," one of the local officers tried to reason with her, but she was having none of it.

"Officer, do you know who I am? I'm Meredith Marsh. My husband built half this town, and I'll be damned if I let you treat my son like a common criminal!" she spat, her eyes narrowing in fury.

Mel exchanged a quick glance with Dana before stepping forward to address the irate woman. "Mrs. Marsh, I understand your concern for your son, but we're just trying to gather information from everyone present during the incident. It's standard procedure, and your son is not being singled out."

Meredith eyed Mel skeptically, trying to gauge her sincerity. She then turned to glare at Blake, as if to place the blame on him for her son's current predicament. "I don't know who you are," she said as she refocused her ire on Mel, "but you better make it quick. I don't want my son associated with this mess any longer than necessary."

"Understood, Mrs. Marsh," Mel replied, her tone remaining professional and even-keeled despite the woman's hostility. She gave Brad an acknowledging nod.

As Meredith moved away from the immediate vicinity, Mel couldn't help but wonder how much of Brad's jealousy and possessiveness stemmed from his mother's influence. With Meredith Marsh now factoring into the equation, the case had gained another layer of complexity.

Mel took a moment to gather her thoughts as she considered the information from both Brad and Blake. She weighed their credibility, motives, and observed their body language. While jealousy could be a powerful motive for Brad, especially given his mother's overbearing nature, Blake's distrust of law enforcement and smarmy demeanor made him difficult to read.

"Hey Mel," Dana said quietly, drawing her out of her thoughts. "So, Elena claimed she was in the bathroom during the blackout. Some of the other guests are saying they saw her go there around that time...er, the time before Slater died."

"Interesting," Mel mused, trying to fit this new piece of information into the puzzle. If Elena's alibi held up, it would weaken Blake's implication of her involvement in Slater's murder. But why did Blake seem so adamant about casting suspicion on Elena?

"Could he be trying to protect himself or someone else?" Mel thought aloud, voicing her doubts about Blake's intentions.

"Maybe," Dana agreed. "Either way, we need to dig deeper into both Brad and Elena's backgrounds. Something just doesn't add up here."

"Agreed," Mel nodded.

As they prepared to continue their investigation, Mel couldn't shake the nagging feeling that there was more to this case than met the eye. The intertwining relationships and potential motives made it difficult to pinpoint who might have had a hand in the murder. With the weight of an unsolved crime hanging over her head, Mel knew she wouldn't rest again until she brought Slater's killer to justice and got Cole in the clear.

CHAPTER 7

M el Crane stormed into the police station, her broad shoulders set with determination. She slammed her badge down on the front desk, startling the officer behind it.

"Sheriff Melissa Crane. Where's my nephew?" she demanded, her voice a mix of steel and fire.

"Uh, Sheriff Crane," the officer stammered, adjusting his glasses nervously. "Cole Crane? I believe he's in the back with his mother, but-"

"Good." Mel cut him off and marched toward the holding cells. The police chief, a portly man with a permanent scowl, appeared in the doorway, trying to block her path.

"Mel, what do you think you're doing?" he growled, crossing his arms over his chest.

"Getting my nephew out of here," she replied without missing a beat. "He's under my protective custody."

"Like hell he is!" the chief spat, his face turning an angry shade of red. "This is my jurisdiction, and I'll handle it how I see fit."

"Try me," Mel challenged, her jaw clenched. They stared each other down, their prior history adding fuel to the fire between them.

"Fine," the chief finally conceded, stepping aside. "But don't think this is over."

"Never thought that for a second," Mel shot back as she moved past him.

Dana sat hunched over her laptop back at the cabin, her fingers flying across the keyboard as she searched for information on Slater, the young woman whose life had been tragically cut short. She scrolled through social media profiles, noting each detail with a frown.

"Come on, there has to be something," she muttered under her breath, clicking on a photo album titled "Maryville Memories." Her eyes widened as she spotted a recurring background in the photos–the inside of a cozy coffee shop near the Maryville College Campus. The location was tagged in a few of the photos.

"Gotcha," she whispered, making a mental note of the location. Slater seemed to be a regular there, and it was worth investigating. But first, she needed Mel and Cole back safely at the cabin.

The crunch of gravel under tires signaled Mel and Cole's arrival at the cabin, drawing the attention of the anxiously waiting family members. Faye, Chloe, Hannah, and Morgan had spent the afternoon preparing a dinner spread to keep their minds off the tense situation while Kris paced the floor, wringing her hands.

"Thank God you're back," Dana said as she rushed out to meet them, relief flooding her features. "Cole, are you okay?"

"Fine, Aunt Dana," Cole replied, trying to muster a reassuring smile but feeling utterly exhausted.

"Let's get everyone inside," Mel announced, ushering the group into the warm glow of the cabin. Once gathered around the table, Faye, Chloe, Hannah, and Morgan presented the feast they'd prepared. As everyone took their seats, Mel stood at the head of the table, commanding their full attention.

"Alright, listen up," she began, her voice firm. "First, thank you for your patience and your support. This whole situation with Cole is...complicated."

Chloe chimed in, her Italian accent thickening with concern, "Mel, we know you're doing everything you can to help him."

"Appreciate that, Chloe," Mel nodded. "And I'm glad you're all here because I need your help, too."

Around the table, everyone exchanged glances.

Mel held up her hands. "I know. I'm usually demanding all of you – some of you more than others – stay out of police business. This is different. The Gatlinburg PD is completely focused on Cole as a suspect. Were we not all here, he'd unfortunately be sitting in a holding cell waiting to be arraigned while they wait on results from the Knoxville crime lab to prove their case."

She glanced at her twin who dabbed at her eyes with a napkin.

"We need to help them see past Cole and start looking at other viable suspects." As the group listened intently, Mel laid out her plan for investigating Slater's murder and uncovering any potential connections to Cole.

"Soon," Mel declared, "we dig deeper. We need to find out more about Slater, her life, and her possible enemies. Someone in that group killed her."

"Absolutely," Faye agreed, determination flashing in her eyes. "We won't let anything happen to Cole."

"Thanks, Mom," Mel replied, touched by her mother's support. Over the years, Faye's friendship with Chloe had broadened her view of the world, making her a staunch ally in their family's quest for truth and justice.

Dana explained how she had found the coffee shop near the college campus where Slater used to hang out.

"That's worth checking out," Mel acknowledged, "but for now everyone, let's just focus on this delicious meal from two world class chefs and two classically trained up and comers, and on being there for Cole. After dinner, we'll tackle this all as a team."

With that, the family dug into their meal, the atmosphere a mix of camaraderie and quiet determination. Mel glanced around at her loved ones, letting a small smile cross her lips. They faced an uphill battle, but they would face it together.

After the meal and a full group effort to speed the cleanup, Mel gathered the family in the living room. "Alright, everyone, we need to get to work. Dana and Lance, you two start researching Brad Marsh and Elena Reyes. Let's see what we can find on them."

"Got it," Dana said, pulling out her laptop.

"Same here," Lance replied, grabbing his tablet.

As they settled onto the couch, Dana began searching for information about Brad. There wasn't much to be found about him, but she quickly discovered that his mother, Meredith, was well known in the community among those who lived there year-round. She was a wealthy real estate agent with a reputation for being ruthless in business.

"Interesting," Dana mused aloud, sharing her findings with Lance. "Meredith Marsh, Brad's mother, has her sights set on any properties along the parkway that come up for sale. She wants all the prime locations for herself."

"Seems like a motive for wanting to discredit Wesley's haunt and take him out of the picture," Lance added thoughtfully.

"Definitely something to consider," Dana agreed. "Let's see what we can find on Elena now."

Lance typed her name into a search engine, and the first result was a website for Elena's CPA business. As they clicked through the site, they discovered an endorsement from Wesley's haunted house where he was reportedly a satisfied customer.

"Looks like Elena has a pretty solid connection to Wesley," Lance pointed out. "Another piece of the puzzle."

"Maybe," Dana acknowledged, "but we'll need more than this to connect her to Slater's murder. We should let Mel know what we've found so far."

"Agreed," Lance said, nodding. "We're only just scratching the surface, but every bit of information helps."

In the background, Mel continued coordinating the family's efforts, assigning tasks and listening intently as each member shared their thoughts and findings.

On Monday afternoon, Dana and Beth visited the coffee shop near the Maryville College campus where Slater used to hang out, hoping to gather more information from her mourning friends. As they entered the cozy establishment, the aroma of freshly brewed coffee enveloped them. They spotted a small group gathered around a corner table, photos of Slater displayed on their phones and in their hands.

"Okay, let's try to blend in," Dana whispered to Beth, who nodded in agreement. They ordered their coffees and found a nearby table, close enough to eavesdrop but not too close to be obvious.

The conversation among Slater's friends was filled with tearful reminiscing and hushed speculation about her death. Dana attempted to steer the discussion towards any potentially helpful information for their investigation nonchalantly, but it proved to be challenging.

"Such a tragedy," Dana interjected when there was a lull in the conversation. "Slater seemed like such a vibrant, outgoing person."

"Yeah, she was," one of Slater's friends replied, eyeing Dana suspiciously. "Do we know you? You don't look familiar."

"Oh, we're just... acquaintances," Beth quickly intervened, trying to salvage the situation. "We met her at a party once."

The group seemed unconvinced, and the atmosphere became noticeably tense. Dana and Beth exchanged glances, understanding that they were outsiders. It was apparent that they wouldn't be able to glean much information from this gathering.

Deciding to cut their losses, Dana and Beth finished their coffees and left the coffee shop. As they walked back to their car, they discussed the limited information they had gathered.

"Looks like we'll have to find another way to dig deeper into Slater's life," Dana sighed, feeling somewhat defeated.

"Maybe someone else in the family will have better luck," Beth suggested, offering a small, supportive smile.

"Let's hope so," Dana replied, her determination renewed. "We're not giving up on this case just yet."

They drove the hour back to the cabin to share their findings with the rest of the family, knowing that each piece of information–no matter how small–could be crucial in unraveling the truth behind Slater's murder.

Later that day, Dana returned to her laptop, her eyes darting back and forth across the screen as she continued to monitor Slater's social media accounts. The evening had settled in, casting shadows across the room and leaving only the glow of the computer screen to illuminate her determined face.

"Hey, I found something," Dana announced, drawing the attention of the Cranes and Rossi family members who were gathered around the dining table, exchanging stories about their day's endeavors.

"What is it?" Marco asked, leaning forward with interest.

"Slater's parents have organized a wake for her tomorrow afternoon," Dana explained, her voice softening out of respect for the deceased. "They posted about it on social media, inviting friends and acquaintances to attend."

"Maybe someone from our family should go," Jesse suggested.

The family members exchanged glances, considering the idea. Faye finally broke the silence, her gaze resolute. "Chloe and I can go," she volunteered. "We've attended wakes before, and we're pretty good at getting people to open up and share their memories."

"Are you sure, Mom?" Mel asked, concern etching her face. "This could be emotionally taxing, especially since we're trying to solve her murder."

Faye gave a reassuring smile. "I can handle it, Mel. Besides, it's important that we use every chance we get to uncover the truth about this case."

"Alright," Mel agreed reluctantly, knowing her mother's determination was unwavering. "But if things become too overwhelming, don't hesitate to leave."

"Of course," Chloe chimed in, placing a supportive hand on Faye's shoulder. "We'll be careful."

As the family continued their discussion, Dana couldn't help but feel a mixture of trepidation and anticipation. Having the moms as she often thought of them attend the wake was a risky move, but it could be crucial for their investigation. She knew Faye and Chloe were capable, but she couldn't shake the nagging worry that something might go wrong.

"Good luck tomorrow," Dana murmured, her fingers tightening around her coffee mug as she silently prayed for their success.

"Thanks, Dana," Faye replied, her eyes reflecting the gravity of the situation. "I hope at least something useful comes of it."

"Let's just hope it brings us one step closer to solving Slater's murder," Marco added.

As the family dispersed for the night, each member felt the weight of their mission bearing down on them. They knew they had to tread carefully, but they also understood the importance of not leaving any stone unturned.

***

The following morning, Faye and Chloe met in Faye and Jesse's room to pick out appropriate attire for the wake. They wanted to balance blending in and showing respect while maintaining the guise of acquaintances.

"Maybe I should wear this black dress," Chloe suggested, holding up a simple yet elegant piece that fell just below her knees. "I brought it in case we went out anywhere fancy. It's not too flashy, but it still looks respectful."

"Good choice," Faye agreed, selecting a dark gray dress from what she'd brought. "I brought this along for the same reason, though Jesse isn't big on fancy restaurants and such. It should work just fine for a wake, too. We don't want to draw too much attention to ourselves."

As they dressed, the two women discussed the strategy for handling questions about their relationship to Slater. They knew they had to come up with a convincing story that wouldn't arouse suspicion.

"Let's say we knew her through a great niece who was a classmate of hers at college," Faye proposed, adjusting the collar of her blouse. "We can mention that we're both from Knoxville and we heard about her passing through the grapevine."

"Sounds plausible," Chloe approved, nodding as she slipped on her dress. "And if anyone asks why we didn't know her better, we can say that our paths didn't cross often, but we felt it was important to pay our respects."

"Exactly," Faye said, satisfaction evident in her voice. "Hopefully, that will be enough to satisfy any curiosity."

With their outfits selected and their cover story decided, Faye and Chloe took one last look in the mirror, ensuring their appearance was suitable for the solemn occasion. Though they were unsure of what information they would uncover, they were determined to do everything in their power to help solve Slater's murder.

"Alright," Chloe sighed, taking a deep breath as she clasped her hands together. "Are you ready to do this?"

"Yes," Faye responded firmly, her eyes filled with resolve.

With that, the two women left the cabin, ready to face whatever challenges awaited them at the wake.

As Faye and Chloe stepped out of the cabin, they steeled themselves for what lay ahead.

"Remember," Chloe said, her voice steady as they climbed into the car, "our goal is to gather information. Let's not draw too much attention to ourselves."

"Agreed," Faye nodded, starting the engine. "The more we blend in, the better our chances of finding something useful."

The drive to the wake was filled with tense anticipation. Both women were lost in thought, mentally rehearsing their cover story and preparing for questions that might come their way.

Upon arriving at the family home, Faye and Chloe took a moment to collect themselves before stepping inside. The house was brightly lit but the mood was somber. The scent of fresh flowers filled the air, creating an atmosphere of reverence and quiet reflection.

"Stay close," Faye whispered to Chloe as they made their way through the crowd of mourners. "And remember, we're here to listen and observe."

They skipped signing the guest book, but while they waited in a short line to offer their condolences to Slater's family, Faye and Chloe kept their ears open for any snippets of conversation that could prove helpful in their investigation. They listened carefully, hoping that among the whispers of sympathy and shared memories, they might find a clue that would lead them closer to the truth behind Slater's untimely death.

CHAPTER 8

The mournful chatter of the wake filled the modest living room, creating a thick fog of grief that hung over the gathering. Faye and Chloe exchanged glances, their eyes darting between the guests and Heidi, Slater's mother who still stood near the foyer, greeting mourners as they entered the family home.

The moms moved through the crowd, offering condolences to other mourners in distress while waiting for an opportunity to speak with Heidi alone.

Chloe grabbed Faye's elbow. "Excuse us," she whispered as she gently nudged a distant aunt out of the way. To Faye she said, Heidi is on the move.

Making their way towards the younger woman, they found her standing near the dining table, clutching a tissue in one hand and a glass of ice water in the other.

"Mrs. Walker," Faye began softly, causing Heidi to turn her tear-streaked face towards them. "Again, we're so sorry for your loss."

"Thank you," Heidi murmured, dabbing at her eyes with the tissue. "I appreciate it." She glanced around the crowded room. "It's just...it's all happened so fast."

"Actually, that's what we wanted to talk to you about," Chloe said, glancing at Faye for support. "Why was the wake organized so quickly? Why, you've hardly had time to process what's happened."

Heidi hesitated, looking around the room once more before lowering her voice. "Well, you see, a lot of our family members were already in town for Spring Break. We thought it would be best to hold the wake now, while everyone is here."

"Ah, I see," Faye replied, nodding her understanding. Inwardly, she wondered if there was more to the story than Heidi was letting on. The atmosphere in the room seemed strained, as if the hurried preparations had left everyone feeling off-balance.

"Was that the only reason?" Chloe asked delicately. She caught Faye's eye, sharing her concerns about the underlying tension at the wake.

Heidi sighed, shifting her weight from one foot to the other. "To be honest, we didn't want to drag it out any longer than necessary. Having everyone here for Spring Break...it just made sense."

"Of course," Faye said sympathetically, placing a comforting hand on Heidi's arm. "It must be incredibly difficult for you and your family right now."

"Thank you," Heidi whispered, her voice cracking with emotion. She took a shaky breath before excusing herself to greet another guest.

As Faye and Chloe watched her walk away, they shared a look of concern. The hurried wake and the tension in the room left them with more questions than answers. They knew they had to dig deeper.

As they moved through the crowded room, Faye noticed a young woman standing near the corner, watching the interactions with keen interest. She nudged Chloe and nodded toward the woman. "Let's see if she knows anything."

"Good idea," Chloe agreed, and they approached the woman, who appeared to be in her late twenties.

"Excuse me," Faye said, offering a warm smile. "I'm Faye, and this is Chloe. We're friends of Slater's parents. You look like you might be related?"

The woman returned the smile, albeit a bit hesitantly. "Yes, I'm Slater's cousin, Kelsey. It's nice to meet you both."

"Likewise," Chloe replied. "We were just talking to Heidi about the wake. Such a tragedy what happened to Slater."

Kelsey's expression darkened. "Yes, it's awful. And so unexpected."

"Did you know Slater well?" Faye asked gently.

"Fairly well," Kelsey admitted. "We weren't as close as we used to be, but we still talked from time to time. We kind of parted ways while she was with Renee, Wesley's daughter."

"Wesley Collins?" Faye asked.

"Yes."

"Slater and Renee were together?" Chloe asked."

"Yes," Kelsey said, nodding slowly. "That caused some tension between them; between Slater and Wesley, I mean, especially since Slater was working for Wesley at the haunted house. He didn't approve of their relationship at all."

"Really? Why not?" Faye pressed, sensing that there was more to the story.

"From what I heard, Wesley thought Slater was flighty and unreliable. He didn't think she was good enough for his daughter," Kelsey explained, her voice dropping into a whisper. "His daughter though, was in love with Slater. She even asked her to marry her at one point."

"Wow," Chloe murmured, exchanging a significant glance with Faye. "That must have caused quite a stir."

Kelsey nodded. "It did. But Slater said no. She told Renee she was going back to school. After that, she started dating men again."

Faye glanced around the crowded room. "That must have angered Wesley even more."

"Definitely a motive for resentment," Chloe concurred, nodding thoughtfully.

"Yeah, Wesley was pretty mad, and it strained his relationship with Renee. It's...well, it's just so sad that things never got resolved between Slater and Renee, and Slater and Wesley before...before this happened."

"Indeed," Faye agreed solemnly, the weight of Kelsey's revelations settling heavily upon her. She and Chloe thanked Kelsey for talking with them and moved away to process the information they had just learned.

"Interesting, isn't it?" Chloe mused. "The tension between Wesley and Slater could've played a role in what happened."

"Maybe," Faye agreed cautiously, not yet ready to jump to conclusions.

As they continued to observe the wake attendees, Faye's gaze landed on a tall, thin man with hawkish features who had just entered the room. She nudged Chloe subtly and nodded in his direction.

"Isn't that Devon?" she asked quietly, trying not to draw attention to themselves.

"Looks like it," Chloe confirmed, her expression turning serious. "What do you think he's doing here?"

"Let's find out," Faye suggested, her curiosity piqued by Devon's unexpected appearance. As they made their way over to him, she couldn't help but feel that the puzzle pieces surrounding Slater's death were gradually falling into place.

"Devon," Chloe greeted him with a friendly smile, hoping to put him at ease. "We didn't expect to see you here."

Recognition dawned in his eyes. "Slater and I were, uh...we were friends," Devon admitted, though his voice lacked warmth, and his eyes darted around the room nervously. "I wanted to pay my respects."

"Of course," Faye said, sympathetically. "It's a difficult time for everyone."

As they exchanged pleasantries, Faye and Chloe couldn't shake the feeling that there was more to Devon's presence at the wake than met the eye.

Chloe plunged in first. "Devon," she began, being careful not to sound accusatory, "could you tell us a bit more about your connection with Slater? We're trying to understand what happened."

"Slater and I worked on a few projects together," Devon replied, his gaze flickering between Faye and Chloe. "Nothing too serious, just some stuff for the haunted house."

"Can you give us some examples?" Faye asked, her curiosity growing.

"Uh, well," Devon hesitated, rubbing the back of his neck. His eyes darted around the room again, as if searching for an escape route. "You know, just some electronic installations, that kind of thing."

"She had an electrical background?" Faye probed.

"No. Not exactly. She was an employee in the haunted house, is all. A pair of hands that helped with the setup of new installations."

"Did you ever have any conflicts with her?" Chloe inquired, sensing Devon's increasing discomfort.

"Look," Devon said, the tension in his voice rising, "I really don't see how this is relevant right now. We're here to mourn Slater, not dig into her past."

"Of course," Faye agreed quickly, trying to placate him. "We're just trying to get a clearer picture of who she was. It might help us all come to terms with her loss."

"Sorry," Devon muttered, his face flushed with irritation. "I can't help you. Excuse me." And without another word, he slipped away from them and disappeared into the crowd.

Faye and Chloe exchanged frustrated glances, both realizing that they had hit a dead end with Devon. His evasive answers and sudden disappearance only heightened their suspicions.

They turned their attention back to the wake, where they now knew what some of the tension was that hung in the air. It was almost palpable, the tension, the way it added an uneasy weight to the overall atmosphere.

Faye noticed Wesley had arrived at some point. She tugged Chloe into a corner, out of his line of sight, then pointed him out. "We probably should leave. He could blow our cover."

"Look at him," Chloe whispered to Faye, nodding discreetly towards Wesley. "He's practically radiating anger." Wesley seemed to avoid making eye contact with anyone connected to Slater, his jaw clenched tight as he nursed a glass of whiskey he'd apparently poured himself from bottles Slater's parents had set out for the mourners.

"Can't blame him entirely, considering the circumstances," Faye replied, her eyes narrowing as she studied his body language. "But it doesn't help the situation."

Faye watched too as Slater's parents stood in the corner, hands clasped together like a lifeline. The tension within the room continued to be an almost tangible presence–a reminder of the unsolved murder that had shattered their world.

"Look at them," Chloe muttered, following Faye's gaze. "They're barely holding it together."

"Can you blame them?" Faye replied softly, her eyes never leaving the grieving couple. "Their daughter's death has turned their lives upside down."

Around them, family members continued to whisper and exchange wary glances. It was obvious the strain of the situation had seeped into every conversation, casting a dark cloud over the gathering.

"Come on," Faye whispered to Chloe as they stepped away from the gathering. "Let's give them all some space."

As they exited the wake, being careful to avoid Wesley spotting them, the amateur detectives felt the weight of unanswered questions pressing heavily on their shoulders.

As they stepped outside, Faye took a deep breath of the crisp mountain air, grateful for the temporary reprieve from the heavy atmosphere within. They climbed into their car and drove back to the cabin in silence, each lost in her own thoughts about the case.

Upon arriving, Faye and Chloe found Mel, Dana, Jesse, Marco, Kris, and Lance gathered around the living room, eager for an update. In the all-seasons room, the younger folks splashed in the pool, trying to maintain a sense of normalcy for Cole's sake.

"Find out anything?" Mel asked, her voice betraying her concern.

Faye took a seat, but Chloe stayed on her feet as she spoke. "Slater had a rocky history with Wesley," Chloe began, recounting the details of the tumultuous relationship. "Wesley didn't approve of her dating his daughter, which eventually led to further tensions between them."

"Did anyone else seem suspicious?" Lance inquired, leaning forward in his seat.

"Devon showed up unexpectedly," Faye added, furrowing her brow. "He was evasive when we tried to question him and then disappeared. We couldn't get much out of him." She told them all what little he had said.

"Sounds like we have more digging to do," Dana mused, her eyes narrowing in determination.

"Definitely," Faye agreed. "But for now, let's focus on supporting Cole."

"Anything from the Gatlinburg police?" Chloe asked.

Mel shook her head. "Nothing. We don't know much, but unless they had someone at that wake too, I'm guessing we know more than they do."

Marco, ever the police lieutenant even in retirement, put in, "We should probably let the Gatlinburg PD know what we know. It might speed up the process of clearing Cole, if nothing else."

Mel nodded. "You're right, as much as I hate the thought of helping them when they couldn't be bothered to help me." She let out a huff of air. "Why don't we go into town tomorrow and have a sit down with them?" She looked at her father-in-law. "Will you come, Marco? Be a buffer of sorts?"

"Of course."

CHAPTER 9

M el shifted her weight on the bed, the sheets rustling softly in the quiet room. She could feel Dana's warmth pressed against her side as they lay facing each other, their legs entwined beneath the covers. The soft glow of the bedside lamp cast shadows on the ceiling, creating an intimate atmosphere for their late-night conversation.

"Something just doesn't add up," Mel said, her lips twisting into a scowl as she thought about the murder case. "I can't shake the feeling that Wesley isn't our guy."

Dana sighed and propped herself up on one elbow, her brown hair falling across her face. "You're right. It's too easy to pin it all on him because of his connection to Slater and the haunted house. But what about Devon?"

"Devon?" Mel repeated, considering the possibility. She remembered Faye and Chloe saying he had turned up at the wake. Even though their moms seemed skeptical about his explanation, they all knew he had sold animatronics to Wesley for his haunt. His story of working with Slater during installs was plausible on the surface. "He could've had access to Wesley's haunted house and all the equipment, not just the extra stuff he brought in for the demo...but do we have any evidence to suggest he's involved?"

"Nothing concrete," Dana admitted, running a hand through her hair. "But we can't rule him out just because we don't have enough proof yet." As she spoke, her fingers traced small circles on Mel's shoulder, a comforting gesture that kept them connected even as they delved into the unsettling details of the case.

"Agreed," Mel said, her mind racing with potential theories and connections. "We need to keep digging, Dana. There has to be something we're missing."

"Tomorrow we'll go over everything again," Dana suggested, her voice soft but determined. "We'll retrace our steps, talk to more people, and see if any new leads come up. We can't let this case go cold, Mel."

"Absolutely," Mel agreed, her jaw set in determination.

"Speaking of which," Dana continued, "we haven't talked much about Elena Reyes. We know her connection to Wesley. Could she have been connected to Slater? The information we've gathered about her isn't very consistent either. She's a CPA, but she's only part time down here and part time in Ohio. Why come to a haunted house event? What was her angle? And why on earth come with Blake, but I digress!"

"She's a CPA. Could she have been involved in the finances for Wesley's haunted house more than just doing the books?" Mel wondered aloud, trying to piece together a connection between the two. "If that's the case, maybe there's something going on with the money that we don't know about yet."

"Or maybe her connection to Wesley was more personal," Dana suggested, her eyes narrowing as she weighed the possibilities. "We need to find out more about her past, especially during her time in

Tennessee. Maybe there's something there that can help us understand her relationship with Wesley."

"Right," Mel agreed. "I'll reach out to Blake tomorrow. He might have some information about Elena and her involvement with Wesley."

"Be careful with him, though," Dana warned. "You know better than anyone that he's not the most reliable source. Why don't I fill Yvonne in and see if she'll let me run some background checks on Elena, Brad, and Devon? That should give us more concrete information to work with."

"That's a good idea if she'll allow it," Mel said, giving Dana a determined nod. "And let's not forget about Meredith. She has an obvious motive for wanting Wesley out of the picture. That haunted house he owns is sitting on prime real estate, and his building could have a lot of value, too, as something other than a haunt. Meridith's been trying to get her hands on everything along there for quite some time, it appears."

"True," Dana said. "From what we know, Meredith might do almost anything to own that property, even if it meant manipulating her own son."

"Exactly," Mel affirmed. "If Brad was her hitman in all this, it would discredit Wesley and likely force him to sell the property. She'd finally get what she wanted."

"Ugh, the thought of a mother using her own son like that... it's just so twisted." Dana shuddered. But despite the disturbing nature of their theory, it made more sense in a morbid way.

"Twisted or not, we need to consider every possibility," Mel stated. "We can't ignore any potential leads, no matter how dark they are."

"Agreed," Dana sighed. "Tomorrow, let's follow up on these leads and see where they take us. And maybe dad is right. It's time we looped in the police; we might help expedite their investigation and get Cole cleared."

Mel concurred. "We'll all regroup first thing in the morning and start making some calls."

CHAPTER 10

Cole Crane tapped his foot impatiently, the wooden floorboards of the cabin creaking in protest. Through the dust-speckled windows, he could see the sun climbing higher in the cloudless sky. He sighed, running a hand through his unruly hair as he paced back and forth inside the cramped living room.

"Come on, Beth," he urged, turning to his sister who was comfortably sprawled on the worn-out couch, her nose buried in a book. "Half the day is gone. I can't stand being cooped up in here any longer."

Beth glanced up from her novel, annoyance flashing in her eyes. "It's not that bad, Cole. Besides, you're supposed to be lying low for a while."

"Exactly," he grumbled, hands shoved deep into his pockets. "lying low doesn't mean we have to waste away in this cabin. We could at least go out to Pigeon Forge or something."

"Fine," she conceded, snapping her book shut with an exaggerated sigh. "But you know Aunt Mel won't let us go alone."

"Then we'll just have to find someone else to tag along," he said, a mischievous glint in his eyes.

As if on cue, the front door swung open, revealing Grandpa Jesse. His weathered face broke into a smile when he saw his two grandchildren. "What's all this commotion about?" he asked, wiping sweat from his brow from an hour rocking on the porch, in the sun.

"Perfect timing, Grandpa!" Cole exclaimed, wrapping an arm around the old man's shoulders. "Beth and I were just discussing our need for some fresh air and adventure, and we thought maybe you'd like to join us on a little outing to Pigeon Forge?"

Grandpa Jesse raised an eyebrow, amused by his grandson's sudden enthusiasm. "Well now, aren't you supposed to stay here? What exactly do you two have in mind?"

"Nothing too crazy," Beth chimed in, hopping off the couch and joining her brother and grandfather. "Maybe some go-karts, an arcade... Just something to get us out of the house for a bit. He just has to have adult supervision at all times. That's where you come in."

The old man considered their proposal, glancing between his eager grandchildren. He knew how much they needed this break from the suffocating stillness of the cabin. "Alright," he finally agreed, chuckling. "But only if I get to show you youngsters how it's done on the go-kart track."

"Deal!" Cole grinned, excitement coursing through him at the prospect of escaping the confines of the cabin. Adventure awaited them in Pigeon Forge.

Grandpa Jesse handed Cole the car keys, and with a wink, said, "You can drive, but don't get us into any trouble."

"Of course not, Grandpa," Cole replied, pocketing the keys. He could feel the weight of responsibility and trust placed upon him.

The trio arrived at the bustling arcade and go-kart venue, the air thick with excitement and laughter. The scent of popcorn and cotton candy filled their nostrils as they stepped out of the car.

"Alright, let's head inside!" Beth suggested, her eyes wide with anticipation.

"Right behind you," Cole agreed, locking the car and pocketing the keys once more.

As they entered the arcade, Cole and Beth led Grandpa Jesse to a comfortable seat near the entrance, where he could relax and watch the action unfold. They promised to return shortly after checking out the games and grabbing some tokens.

Wandering through the rows of arcade machines, Cole and Beth's attention was suddenly drawn to the ice cream stand. They talked about getting milk shakes, then they spotted Devon and Brad standing in line, engaged in what appeared to be a serious conversation.

"Isn't that Brad?" Beth whispered to Cole, nodding towards the pair. "And who's that guy with him? I think I've seen him before."

"Yeah, that's definitely Brad," Cole confirmed, his curiosity piqued. "And the other guy looks familiar to me too, but I'm not sure who he is." He studied Devon's tall, thin frame, and the hawkish intensity of his features. "I'm pretty sure he was at the haunted house."

"Let's hang back and see what we can find out," Beth suggested, her voice barely audible. "Something seems off about this."

Cole agreed, and together they watched from a discreet distance, their ears straining to pick up any clues why Brad was conversing with this mysterious man they were both sure they'd seen before, too.

"Alright, let's not make it obvious," Cole whispered, leading Beth to a nearby Skee-ball game. They pretended to play while watching Brad and Devon.

As the pair got their ice cream and walked away from the counter, Cole and Beth stealthily followed them, careful not to be spotted. The murmur of the arcade machines provided enough cover for their footsteps as they closed in on the conversation between Brad and Devon.

"Listen, Devon," Brad said cautiously, "it's important that you meet my mother, Meredith. She's got the connections we need to pull off the plan."

"Are you sure she'll be on board with this?" Devon asked skeptically, taking a bite of his ice cream cone.

"Trust me," Brad replied with a grin. "She's always looking for ways to expand her real estate empire. This will be right up her alley."

Cole and Beth exchanged glances, their hearts pounding with intrigue. What was "the plan" that Brad and Devon were discussing, and how did Meredith Marsh fit into the equation? Their curiosity now thoroughly piqued, they knew they couldn't let this opportunity slip by without finding out more.

"Let's keep following them," Cole mouthed to Beth, his eyes never leaving the two men as they continued to walk through the arcade. Beth nodded, her expression determined, and together they trailed Brad and Devon like shadows.

"Alright, we'll meet at my mom's house in an hour," Brad said to Devon as they neared the entrance of the arcade. "Just remember to play it cool and act like you're interested in her real estate business. She can't know what we're really up to."

"Got it," Devon replied with a nod, before disappearing into the bustling Pigeon Forge crowd outside.

As Brad walked away in the opposite direction, Cole turned to Beth, his eyes wide with anticipation. "We have to see what's going on at Meredith's place."

"Are you sure that's a good idea?" Beth asked hesitantly, glancing back at the arcade where their grandpa sat, snoozing in his seat.

"Grandpa Jesse will be fine. He won't even notice we're gone," Cole assured her, as he fingered the car keys in his pocket. "Besides, if we don't follow them now, we might never get another chance to find out what they're plotting. We've both heard the adults talking. This may be something that helps them figure everything out."

After a moment of consideration, Beth nodded, her curiosity winning over any lingering doubts. "Okay, let's do it. But we have to be careful not to get caught."

"Agreed," Cole said, leading the way out of the arcade.

They hurried to the parking lot and climbed into their grandpa's car. Cole started the engine quickly. With hearts pounding and adrenaline rushing through their veins, the two siblings set off to follow Brad towards Meredith Marsh's house, determined to uncover the mysterious plan between Brad and Devon.

As Brad slowed and pulled into the driveway of a massive home, Cole slowed down in his grandfather's 'Sunday' car, the one he drove to church and when they had to go into the city, like to Columbus, and parked a safe distance away. A grand estate loomed in front of them, its imposing structure casting shadows over the neatly trimmed lawn.

"Stay low," Cole whispered to Beth as they hunched down in their seats, peering through the car windows at Brad pacing back and forth outside the house talking on his phone.

"Who do you think he's talking to?" Beth asked, her voice barely audible as she observed Brad holding his phone to his ear. His agitated movements implied the conversation wasn't going well.

"Probably his mom or Devon," Cole guessed, his gaze never leaving Brad. "He seems pretty mad."

Minutes ticked by, and it was clear Brad's frustration was mounting. He broke off the call and tried dialing again only, it appeared to the kids, to receive no answer. Brad's jaw clenched, and he kicked at a stone on the walkway, sending it skittering across the pavement.

Brad stormed into the house.

"Something's definitely off," Cole remarked, his instincts screaming that this situation was far from ordinary. "I don't like this, Beth. I think we need to find out what's happening inside that house."

Beth hesitated, biting her lip nervously. "But if we get caught..."

"Then we'll say we were worried about my case and thought we heard something suspicious," Cole interjected, his determination unwavering. "We can't let this go, Beth. We may not get another chance."

Taking a deep breath, Beth finally nodded. "Alright, let's do it. But we have to be quick and quiet."

"Agreed," Cole said, his heart racing with excitement and anxiety. As they exited the car and crept towards the house, the siblings could feel the tension building in the air.

Before they could even reach the door, it swung open abruptly, and Brad reappeared. He glanced around nervously before rushing back to his car at a pace that bordered on frantic. The engine roared to life, and he sped off down the street without sparing another moment.

"Come on," Cole urged, tugging Beth's hand as they dashed towards the now-open front entrance. They slipped inside, trying to ignore the sense of unease settling in their stomachs.

The house was eerily quiet. Their footsteps seemed to echo through the empty front hallway as they cautiously ventured further in. Cole's heart pounded in his chest, but he refused to let fear deter him from uncovering the truth. Beth clung to his arm, her own nerves stretched thin but trusting her brother's determination.

As they rounded a corner towards the living room, they discovered the source of the unsettling atmosphere. A woman lay sprawled on the floor, surrounded by shattered glass and flowers from a vase. Her eyes were wide with shock, and a pool of blood had spread beneath her motionless form.

Cole's breath caught in his throat, and his grip on Beth tightened. Fear and an overwhelming sense of urgency drove them forward, knowing that time was of the essence if they were to figure out what had happened here and how it connected to their own investigation.

"Is she...?" Beth whispered, her voice trembling.

"Dead," Cole confirmed grimly. "We need to call Aunt Mel, now."

Beth's emotional reaction to the traumatic sight hit her like a tidal wave. Her chest tightened, and she hyperventilated as tears welled up in her eyes. She couldn't tear her gaze away from the lifeless body on the floor, sobbing uncontrollably as the shock overwhelmed her.

"Hey, hey," Cole whispered urgently, wrapping an arm around his sister's shoulders. "We need to keep it together, okay? We'll get through this." His voice was steady and determined, even as his own heart raced with fear.

He pulled out his phone and dialed Aunt Mel's number, hoping that she'd have some insight into the situation. The line rang once, twice, before she picked up. "Mel Crane," came her brisk response, echoing her usual professional demeanor.

"Aunt Mel, it's Cole," he said quickly, struggling to keep his voice steady. "Listen, we're at Meredith's house, and there's... there's a dead woman on the floor. We don't know what happened, but we think it might be connected to Brad and Devon's plan."

"Slow down, Cole," Aunt Mel instructed, concern lacing her tone. "You're where?"

"Meredith Marsh's house. It's a long story, but someone is dead here."

"You and Beth need to get out of there immediately. Touch nothing else, and I'll come over as soon as I can. This could be a crime scene–do you understand?"

"Y-yeah," Cole stammered, his resolve wavering for the first time since entering the house. "We understand. We'll wait outside."

"Do you know where exactly you are?"

"No, not really, but Mom has GPS tracking on my phone she can see from hers. She...she doesn't always trust me."

"That's probably a good thing, in this case," Mel replied, her voice stern but comforting all at once. She motioned to Kris who hurried over to her. "I'm on my way. I'll call the police on the way, okay? If they get there first, stay right out front where they can see you when they get there and do what they say."

"Okay." Cole swallowed hard, ended the call, and turned to console his distraught sister. Cole's heart pounded as he pocketed his phone, the urgency in Aunt Mel's voice ringing in his ears. He glanced at Beth, her face pale and tear-streaked, her chest heaving with each ragged breath.

"Come on," he murmured, taking her hand. "Let's get out of here."

As they retraced their steps through the house, Cole couldn't help but feel a chill creeping down his spine. The dimly lit rooms seemed to close in around them, shadows lurking in every corner. He could practically feel the oppressive energy of the crime scene, its secrets begging to be uncovered.

"Almost there," he whispered to Beth, squeezing her hand reassuringly. She nodded, her wide eyes fixed on the exit.

They finally reached the front door, and Cole pushed it open with a trembling hand. The cool March air washed over them like a balm, offering a brief reprieve from the stifling atmosphere inside.

As they waited for their aunt to arrive, the weight of their situation sank in, and the unanswered questions loomed even larger in their minds. Cole knew he was in a lot of trouble.

"Wait here," Cole instructed, trying to sound more composed than he felt. He eyed the car keys in his hand, contemplating whether to fetch Grandpa Jesse from the arcade or stay put. But Aunt Mel's words echoed in his mind - stay safe, alright?

"Are we just going to leave her... like that?" Beth choked out between sobs, her gaze darting back towards the house.

"We have to," Cole replied, his voice firm despite the uneasiness gnawing at him. "Aunt Mel will handle it. We can't risk contaminating the scene."

Still clutching his sister's hand, they retreated to the edge of the yard, watching the dark windows of Meredith's house with trepidation. Cole's thoughts raced, questions swirling like a torrent: What was Brad's plan? Who killed the woman inside? And most how did this murder connect to the first one?

As they waited in tense silence, the minutes stretched into what felt like hours, but neither Cole nor Beth could tear their gaze away from the house, as if expecting an answer to materialize before them.

Finally, the sound of a car approaching pierced through the silence, heralding Aunt Mel's arrival. As she stepped out of her car, determination etched on her face, Cole couldn't help but feel a flicker of hope - maybe, just maybe, they were one step closer to unraveling the mystery that had ensnared them.

But for now, all they could do was wait and watch as their aunt strode towards the house, leaving them both shrouded in uncertainty and fear.

CHAPTER 11

The fluorescent lights flickered overhead as Beth and Cole were forcefully guided into separate interrogation rooms. The sterile, windowless chambers only heightened the tension that had been building since their arrival at the police station. Each room held a single metal table, bolted to the floor, with two chairs on either side. Both siblings sat down, their hands cuffed behind their backs, their expressions a mixture of fear and defiance.

"Why aren't you waiting for lawyers?" Kris demanded, her voice echoing off the cold, concrete walls. She stood between the two rooms, her eyes darting back and forth between her children. "My kids have rights!"

"Kris, we'll get them an attorney," Mel said, her voice strained as she tried to maintain some semblance of control over the situation. As a sheriff, she was used to being the one in charge, but this case hit too close to home. Her broad shoulders tensed, betraying her own anxiety.

"We're calling the public defender's office now," an officer said.

"Damn right you are!" Kris snapped, her frustration palpable. She couldn't believe her own sister would allow this to happen to her family. "And I want to be in there with them! You can't just leave them alone like this!"

"Kris, you can't be in both rooms," Mel sighed, rubbing her temples. "You know how these things work. I'll sit in with Cole to keep him in check until a lawyer gets here." She knew her nephew had a tendency to let his emotions take over, and she feared what he might say without someone there to guide him through the process.

"Fine," Kris relented, though her tone made it clear this wasn't a battle she was willing to lose entirely. "But I'm not leaving this station until they're out of those damn rooms!"

As Kris stood her ground, Mel entered the room where Cole sat, his eyes red and puffy from unshed tears. She could see the veins in his neck throbbing as he clenched his jaw, trying to hold himself together.

"Hey, buddy," she said softly, taking the seat across from him. "I know this is tough, but we're going to get through it, okay?"

Cole looked up at her, his eyes searching for reassurance. "Aunt Mel," he whispered, his voice cracking with fear, "I didn't do it. I swear. Neither did Beth. It was just like I told you."

"I believe you, Cole," Mel replied, her heart aching for her nephew. "But right now, we need to focus on getting you and Beth out of here, and finding the people who did it."

"Can you promise me something?" Cole asked, his gaze locked on hers.

"Anything."

"Promise me that no matter what happens, you won't let them separate me and Beth. We need each other."

"Cross my heart," Mel promised, her determination renewed. "There's nothing in this world that can break the bond between the Crane family."

As Kris stood outside the interrogation rooms, her hands clenched into fists, she knew that their battle had only just begun. But one thing was certain: they would fight to protect their own.

Just as Mel was about to speak again, Cole's resolve seemed to shatter. He couldn't hold it in any longer. "I have to tell someone," he blurted out. "I can't wait for the attorney. I need to get this off my chest."

"Alright, Cole," Mel said cautiously, trying to keep him calm. "But remember, anything you say can be used against you. So choose your words wisely."

Cole nodded and took a deep breath, then launched into his story. As he spoke, officers and family members in the vicinity gathered around the door of the interrogation room, drawn by the urgency in his voice. Kris and Dana exchanged worried glances but stood close, listening intently.

Meanwhile, in the adjacent room, Beth sat silently, her eyes downcast and her hands fidgeting in her lap.

When Cole finished, Kris and Dana entered Beth's room, hoping to coax the truth from her as well. "Sweetheart," Kris said softly, kneeling beside her daughter. "Your brother is telling the police everything. Now, we need to hear your side of the story, too. It's important that we know the truth so we can help you both."

Beth hesitated, her lower lip quivering with uncertainty. Finally, she looked up at her mother and aunt, tears streaming down her cheeks. "I'll tell you everything," she whispered, her voice trembling. "I just want this nightmare to be over."

As Beth recounted the same series of events that Cole had described, the tension in the room slowly dissipated. It was clear their stories matched, providing them with a solid alibi. Even though their future was still uncertain, it felt like a minor victory in the face of adversity.

Kris wrapped her arms around Beth, holding her tight, while Dana sent a silent prayer of gratitude. Whatever challenges lay ahead, they would face them together, as a family.

An hour later, Detective Harrison gathered the official statements from Beth and Cole. He nodded to Kris and Dana before stepping out of Cole's room, his eyes locked firmly on the files in his hand.

"Alright, let's get moving," he barked to the officers nearby. "We've got matching statements from the Crane kids. Brad and Meredith Marsh are now our primary suspects. I want them found and brought in for questioning, ASAP!"

Amid the ensuing commotion, the station doors swung open, revealing Jesse and Marco with windblown hair and tense expressions. Faye, her face flushed with worry, marched toward her husband, hands on hips.

"Jesse Crane!" she scolded, drawing the attention of those around her. "What on earth were you thinking? Our grandson is sitting here accused of murder, and you're off gallivanting at an arcade instead of keeping your eyes on him?"

"Dammit, Faye," Jesse muttered, his jaw clenched. "I didn't know this would happen. I was just trying to help the boy keep his spirits up."

"Keep spirits up?" Faye snapped, her voice rising. "Our family is falling apart, and you're playing games!"

"Enough, Mom." Mel's voice was firm but gentle. "We need to focus on supporting each other right now."

"Mel's right," Marco chimed in, his deep voice resonating through the crowded hallway. "We need to come together as a family."

Faye's anger softened into worry, her eyes welling up with tears. "I just don't understand how we got here," she whispered, her voice cracking. "How did everything go so wrong?"

"None of us can make sense of it," Dana reassured her, draping an arm around Faye's shoulders. "But we'll get through it. Together."

Meanwhile, Jesse's mind raced with questions and guilt. He rubbed the back of his neck, trying to push away the nagging thoughts.

"Alright, everyone," Detective Harrison announced, interrupting the family's momentary quiet. "We've got teams searching for Brad and Meredith. We'll keep you all informed. In the meantime, let's try to stay calm and focused."

Jesse stared at the polished linoleum floor, his thoughts a stormy tempest. He felt a sudden, sharp pain in his chest, like a vice clamping down on his heart. His breath hitched, and his knees buckled.

"Jesse!" Faye cried out as her husband collapsed to the ground, his face contorted in agony.

"Call an ambulance!" Marco barked, rushing to Jesse's side. The family swarmed around him, panic etched on their faces.

"Stay with us, Dad," Mel urged, her voice wavering. "You're going to be okay."

"Is it his heart?" Kris asked, her eyes wide with fear.

"Feels like it," Jesse gasped, clutching his chest. "Hurts...like hell."

"Damn it, Jesse," Faye whispered, tears streaming down her cheeks, "you stubborn man, you better not leave me now."

"Promise..." he managed, his breaths coming in shallow gulps.

Within a couple of minutes, sirens wailed outside the station. The doors burst open, and a team of paramedics rushed in with a gurney.

"Make way, please!" one of them shouted, expertly navigating through the sea of worried faces.

"Sir, can you tell me what happened?" a young female paramedic asked as they loaded Jesse onto the gurney.

"Ch-chest pains," he stammered, beads of sweat dotting his forehead.

"Alright, we're taking him to the hospital. Who's coming with us?"

"I am," Faye declared, her voice resolute.

"Me too," Chloe chimed in, grabbing her purse. "Marco, get the car."

"We'll be right behind you, Faye," Marco said, his police instincts kicking in.

As the ambulance pulled away from the station, Faye clenched Jesse's hand tightly, her own heart pounding with dread.

Jesse's eyes fluttered closed, his thoughts a mix of guilt and worry.

"Stay with me, Jesse," Faye whispered, her voice breaking. "We need you."

The family watched in anguish as the ambulance disappeared down the street, their hearts heavy with fear and uncertainty. They couldn't shake the feeling that the storm hadn't yet passed—it was only just beginning.

The sterile scent of antiseptic filled the air as Jesse was wheeled through the automatic doors of the emergency room. The overhead lights felt unnaturally bright, casting harsh shadows on the medical staff rushing past Faye. She clutched her purse to her chest, fingers digging into the soft leather as her heart threatened to leap out of her throat.

"Ma'am, you'll need to wait here," a nurse informed Faye, her voice carrying an undertone of sympathy.

"But I want to be with my husband," Faye protested, desperation edging her words.

"Doctor's orders," the nurse replied firmly, but not unkindly. "We'll update you as soon as we can."

Faye reluctantly stepped back, watching helplessly as the doors swung closed behind Jesse and his team of doctors. She sank into a nearby chair, burying her face in her hands as fat tears slid down her cheeks.

"God, please let him be okay," she whispered, her prayers mingling with the hushed conversations around her.

The hospital waiting room felt like a pressure cooker as Marco and Chloe arrived, followed closely by the rest of the family sans the two teenagers, and Dana and Lance. Worried glances were exchanged, and the weight of their collective fear hung heavy in the air.

"Any news?" Mel asked, as she and Kris approached their mother.

"Nothing yet," she choked out, instantly triggering a fresh wave of concern.

"Mom, stay strong," Mel urged, placing a comforting hand on Faye's shoulder. "Dad's tough. He'll pull through this."

"Is there anything we can do?" Kris questioned, her expression haunted by the knowledge that her own children were still at the police station.

"Right now, all we can do is wait and pray," Faye murmured, her eyes glued to the emergency room doors.

As the minutes ticked by, the tension in the room grew palpable. Each time the doors swung open, Faye's heart skipped a beat, only to sink when it wasn't Jesse being wheeled out.

"Damn it," she muttered under her breath, trying to quell the rising panic. "What's taking so long?"

"Mom," Mel said softly, sensing her distress. "We need to trust the doctors. They're doing their best."

"Your father...he promised me he'd be okay," Faye whispered, her eyes glistening with unshed tears. "But what if...?"

"Hey," Chloe interjected, wrapping an arm around Faye's shoulders. "We're all here for you, no matter what happens."

"Thank you," Faye replied, her voice barely audible.

As the family huddled together in the waiting room, each lost in their own thoughts and fears, they couldn't help but feel that their lives had been irrevocably changed. The clock continued to tick away.

Back at the police station, Dana and Lance stood in the hallway outside the interrogation rooms, their eyes darting from one end of the bustling corridor to the other as officers rushed past them. The frenzy of activity was a far cry from the tense silence that had filled the station just an hour before. Now, with Beth and Cole's testimonies in hand, the police were working double-time to locate Brad and Meredith.

"Any news?" Lance asked in a hushed tone, glancing over at Dana.

"Nothing yet," she responded, her fingers tapping nervously on her phone. She was waiting for any updates about their father-in-law, Jesse, but refused to let anxiety get the best of her. "We'll hear something soon, I'm sure."

Lance nodded, his gaze fixed on the door behind which both kids now sat, no doubt still rattled by the day's events. He knew he needed to be strong for his step kids, especially his stepson, but with each passing moment, the weight of uncertainty grew heavier on his shoulders.

"Hey," Dana said, touching Lance's arm gently. "Beth and Cole are going to be okay. We've got their backs, remember?"

"Yeah," Lance muttered, forcing a weak smile. "I know. It's just...everything happening all at once, you know? And Jesse..."

"Jesse's a tough old bird," Dana interjected, trying to quell both their fears. "He'll pull through this, and so will we."

As if on cue, her phone buzzed with a text message. Dana quickly scanned the words, her expression somber as she relayed the information to Lance. "No change in Jesse's condition yet, but they're doing everything they can."

"Let's tell the kids," Lance suggested, swallowing hard. "They deserve to know."

Together, they entered the room where Beth and Cole were waiting, their faces pale and drawn. Dana and Lance shared the update about their grandfather, watching as worry etched itself deeper into the teenagers' features.

"Are they any closer to finding Brad and Meredith?" Beth asked in a shaky voice.

"Hard to say," Dana admitted, her eyes meeting Lance's briefly. "But the police are doing everything they can."

"Damn it," Cole muttered under his breath, clenching his fists. "I just want this to be over."

"Hey," Lance said softly, placing a hand on Cole's shoulder. "We're all in this together. We'll get through it."

As the minutes ticked by, both family groups found themselves caught in a whirlwind of emotions and uncertainty. The clocks seemed to mock them, time moving relentlessly forward with each unanswered question that hung in the air.

CHAPTER 12

J esse Crane lay on the sterile hospital bed, his heart pounding in his chest. The cold air bit at his exposed skin as he clenched his fists, trying to steady his nerves. He didn't like doctors, but he was no stranger to hospitals; years of farming had taken their toll on his body. This time was different. There was a gnawing uncertainty that threatened to engulf him. The doctors had said it was urgent, that they needed to act fast.

"Mr. Crane, we're going to start the procedure soon," a nurse said, her voice kind but firm. She moved around Jesse with calculated precision, attaching wires and tubes to his body. "Just relax and take the deepest breaths you can."

Jesse tried to obey, inhaling through the oxygen mask they had over his nose and mouth as his thoughts drifted to his family. He knew they were worried, waiting just outside those heavy doors. His daughter Mel, who had been so fiercely protective, her twin sister Kris who struggled to balance work, kids, and now this; and his grandchildren, Cole and Beth, who stared at him with wide, innocent eyes. They depended on him, and here he was, helpless.

In the waiting room, the atmosphere was thick with tension. Mel paced the floor like a caged animal, her anxiety mirrored in her sister's eyes. Kris sat with her arms crossed tightly across her chest, alternating worry about her kids back at the police station with worry about her father.

"Mel, honey, you need to sit down," urged her mother-in-law Chloe, her hand reaching out to touch her shoulder.

But Mel shook her head, continuing her relentless pacing. "I can't, Mama Rossi. I just... I can't."

"Maybe we should've insisted they let us bring the kids," Kris muttered. "They should be here. We're a family. We stick together," she insisted, her voice cracking with emotion.

Silence settled over the room as they stared at the clock on the wall, each tick echoing like a hammer against metal. They were all aware of the risks involved in the procedure, but none dared speak it aloud. Instead, their thoughts swirled around the unknown, hoping for the best while bracing for the worst.

"Faye, Mel, Kris," a voice called out, shattering the silence. A doctor stood in the doorway, his face unreadable.

"Is he...?" Mel choked out, her eyes pleading for good news.

The doctor hesitated for a moment before speaking. "We've just started the procedure. It's too early to say anything, but I promise we'll do everything we can for your father."

"Thank you, Doctor," Kris said, her voice strained. The siblings exchanged glances, trying to find reassurance in the other's expression.

As the door closed behind the doctor, Mel finally sank into a chair next to Kris, her head in her hands. The weight of their situation pressed down upon them like a heavy blanket. Jesse was their rock, their foundation. The prospect of losing him was almost too much to bear. Together, they clung to hope and waited anxiously for further news of their father's fate.

"Guys, we need to talk about Slater and Elena," Mel said suddenly, her voice firm. "We can't just sit here and do nothing."

"Mel's right," Kris agreed, her determination shining through the exhaustion in her eyes. "If there's a connection between them, we need to find it and figure out who did this."

The family gathered around the small table in the waiting room, a makeshift war room for their investigation. Mel opened Dana's laptop, pulling up any information they had on Slater and Elena.

"Let's start with the basics," she said. "What do we know about their relationship?"

"Slater was a player," Kris recalled. "She was always flirting with everyone–men, women, it didn't matter. And Elena? She was a lot more reserved. She was pretty and she seemed to have a lot going for her, so her being involved in online dating is a puzzle."

"Could jealousy have been a motive?" Mel suggested, her fingers flailing around on the keyboard as she took notes. Computers were Dana's thing, not hers. "Someone who wanted Elena all to themselves?"

"Or maybe someone who saw Slater as a threat," Kris countered. "Blake, maybe?"

They all contemplated that for a minute, but it just didn't seem fit.

"Maybe it wasn't about their personal lives at all," offered Hannah, who had joined them at the hospital and in their brainstorming session while Morgan minded the toddlers back at the cabin. "Elena was a CPA, right? What if she stumbled onto some kind of financial crime that got her killed?"

"That theory is more plausible," Mel mused, "but we need more concrete evidence to connect either scenario to the murders."

"Let's dig deeper into their backgrounds," Kris proposed. "See if we can find anything that might point us in the right direction."

"Agreed," Mel replied, determination radiating from her. "We owe it to Dad to figure this out. I wish Dana was here because she has access to some things, some databases in particular that I don't have, but let's see what we can do. Let's split up the tasks," she said. "Kris, you look into Elena and Slater's backgrounds. Hannah, focus on any financial irregularities that Elena might have discovered. I'll check on Jesse's condition and then join you two."

"Sounds like a plan," Kris agreed, as they all dispersed to carry out their respective tasks.

***

With the police focused on finding Brad and Meredith and ignoring the kids, Dana and Lance decided it was time to take them to the hospital to see Jesse. The chief didn't fight it.

Lance hustled Beth and Cole into the backseat of the car before he changed his mind, while Dana settled in behind the wheel. They knew how important it was for the children to see their grandfather and offer their support.

As they drove, Dana couldn't help but think about the ongoing manhunt for Brad and Meredith. The urgency to find them and bring them to justice weighed heavily on her mind. She knew how dangerous they could be, especially considering their possible involvement in Slater's murder. She glanced at Lance, who seemed to be lost in thought as well.

"Hey," she said softly, reaching over to squeeze his hand. "We're going to figure this out. They'll find Brad and Meredith, and we'll all get to the bottom of Slater's and Elena's deaths."

Lance returned the squeeze, nodding his agreement. "I know," he replied, his voice firm with determination. "We won't let whoever did this hurt anyone else."

Meanwhile, Mel sat in the hospital waiting room, her mind racing between thoughts of Jesse and the animatronic equipment at the haunted house. Marco had been pestering her to go with him and Dana when she could leave the police station on a mission to get a closer look at Devon's set up and see if it could have possibly caused the blackout that led to Slater's murder, but she was hesitant when they first brought the idea up that morning and she was even more so after all that happened. Her priority was her family and ensuring that Jesse received the best care possible.

"Mel," Marco said, sitting down beside her. "I know you're worried about Jesse, but we really do need your help with the haunted house. There might be a connection between everything going on, and we can't afford to overlook it. I don't think Devon caused the blackout, but given his meeting with Brad today, what if he has something to do with all of this?"

She rubbed her temples, torn between her desire to clear Cole's name once and for all, get justice for Slater and Elena, and her love for her father. "Marco, I understand, but my focus is on my dad right now. I can't just leave him here."

"Mel," he insisted, his voice gentle but firm. "I understand, too, but we don't have much time. Dana is on her way here with Lance and the kids. If there's any chance this is connected, we need to act quickly, before the police release the haunt from crime scene status."

"Do you think the Gatlinburg PD or the Knoxville Crime Lab checked all of that?" Mel asked him.

Marco didn't hesitate. "Do you?" His implication was clear.

Mel looked over at the closed door of the ICU, imagining her father lying unconscious inside. She knew how important it was to uncover the truth behind Slater and Elena's deaths, especially if it could lead them to Brad and Meredith. But could she really leave Jesse's side?

"Alright," she finally agreed, her voice barely above a whisper. "I'll do it, but only because I want answers and closure for all of us. But we need to make this quick. I need to be here for my dad."

"Of course," Marco nodded, understanding the gravity of her decision. "We'll work fast, and hopefully, we'll find something that will lead us closer to the truth."

With that decision made, Mel steeled herself for what lay ahead.

***

The haunted house loomed ominously before them, its dark and twisted exterior casting eerie shadows in the fading twilight. Mel shivered involuntarily as they approached, feeling as though the very air around the place was heavy with tension and dread.

"Creepy place," she muttered under her breath, glancing at Marco who seemed equally unsettled.

"Definitely adds to the atmosphere," he agreed, his eyes scanning the surroundings warily. "Let's get in and out of here as quickly as possible." He punched in a key code he said he got from Wesley the day of their tour when he helped him move something in for Devon.

As they stepped inside, the dim lighting and musty smell only added to the overall sense of unease. The animatronics were silent and still, but Mel couldn't shake the feeling that they were being watched by unseen eyes.

A loud thump caught them all off guard.

Mel drew her backup weapon and called out, "Who's here?"

A man coughed somewhere to their left.

"Police. Identify yourself."

The sound of footsteps approached them. Dana held up her phone with her flashlight app on while she took cover behind a display. Mel stood behind a doorframe on one side, gun raised, while Marco took the other side.

When Devon came into the light, hands raised, Mel lowered her back-up gun and put it back in her ankle holster.

"Devon?" Mel questioned, her tone a mixture of surprise and suspicion. "What are you doing here?"

"Sorry, er, sheriff," Devon replied with an apologetic grimace. "Didn't mean to startle you guys. I got a message from Wesley saying he needed me to pull my display equipment before the police let him reopen tomorrow."

"Odd time to do it," Marco interjected, his eyes narrowing. "Why would he ask you to come here at this hour? And why didn't he meet you here himself?"

"Look, I don't know," Devon said defensively. "I'm just following orders."

The sound of sirens in the distance caught their attention. Before they could react, the door Mel and crew had come through slammed open, revealing Wesley, flanked by two uniformed officers.

"Arrest him!" Wesley barked, pointing at Devon. "He's trying to sabotage my haunted house!"

"Wait, what?" Devon's eyes widened in shock, and he took a step back. "That's not true! I was just—"

"Save it for the judge," one officer said gruffly as he moved forward to handcuff Devon.

Mel exchanged glances with Dana and Marco, all three sensing that something wasn't adding up.

Wesley wasn't done. He jabbed a finger toward Devon. "He wants my haunted house." Then he turned to Marco. "And why are you here? You working with him, or do you want my haunted house too? Arrest them all," he commanded the two patrol officers. "They're all trespassing."

"Enough!" Mel snapped, stepping between Wesley and Marco. "We're all here to figure out what's going on with these murders and how they might be connected to your haunted house. If you want this mess cleared up, we need to work together."

Wesley's face contorted in anger before he crossed his arms and huffed. "Fine. But I still say Devon's up to no good."

"Let's just take a step back for a moment," Dana suggested, her voice calm but assertive. "Devon, can you explain why you were removing your equipment?"

"Like I said," Devon began, visibly struggling to keep his composure as the officer held him firmly. "Wesley sent me a message asking me to remove my display equipment from the haunted house." Keeping one arm in the air, he pulled out his phone with his other hand. He asked the officer holding his other arm to release him for a moment. When the officer did, Devon tapped the screen and held his phone out to Dana. "It's right there. He didn't give me a reason, and I don't have any motive to sabotage anything!"

"Is that true, Wesley?" Marco asked, his tone skeptical. "Did you send him a message?"

"Of course not!" Wesley spat, glaring at Devon. "He's lying! This whole thing is a setup!"

Dana passed the phone to an officer. "There's a message there and it appears to be from Wesley."

"Okay, let's all just take a breath," Mel interjected, her mind racing to make sense of the conflicting stories. "If you didn't send the message, Wesley, then someone else did. Someone who wants us to believe Devon is responsible for sabotaging your haunted house."

"Or maybe it was an inside job," Dana added, a glint of suspicion in her eyes. "You could've staged this whole scene to throw us off track."

"Me? Why would I do that?" Wesley demanded, his face reddening.

"Because you're hiding something," Marco accused, taking a step closer to Wesley. "Something about your haunted house that connects it to the murders, and you don't want us digging around."

"Enough!" Mel shouted, her voice echoing through the haunted house. "We're getting nowhere with these accusations. We need to find the real culprit, and we'll start by tracking down who sent that message to Devon."

"Fine," Wesley said begrudgingly, still glaring at Marco. "But I'm going to be watching all of you right back."

The two patrol officers exchanged glances. One asked, "Are you all PI's or something?"

"They're interlopers," Wesley threw out.

Mel realized they were dealing with night shift officers who had played no role she was aware of in either case the previous few days. She took out her badge wallet. "I'm Sheriff Melissa Crane from Muskingum County, Ohio. This is my wife Dana, a retired Customs and Border Patrol investigator, and her father Marco, a retired lieutenant with the Pittsburgh PD. We came down here for a vacation and got involved in a murder investigation because my nephew Cole is...was a prime suspect in the death of Slater Walker."

"Maybe you all better come with us too," the taller of the two young officers said. "Wasn't that kid brought back in today?"

"What kid?" Wesley asked.

"Cole Crane," the shorter officer answered.

Mel watched Wesley's eyes narrow. He worked his mouth before asking the question most people would have asked straight away. "For what?"

"There's been another murder."

"I see. And he's suspected of that too?"

The two patrolmen looked at each other. The shorter one shrugged, giving the taller one tacit permission to speak.

"Not suspected, I believe. He's a witness."

Mel watched Wesley again. Other than an eye twitch, he showed no sign the information affected him.

"Let's go everyone," the tall guy said. He looked at Mel. "Do you have a vehicle here?"

"Of course."

"I expect we can trust you to follow us down to the station. We'll get everyone's statement there. Mr. Collins here can decide who he's pressing charges against, if anyone. Sounds like a big mess."

"Again, of course."

The shorter guy piped up. "We should read them all their rights."

Mel spoke for her group saying, "We waive them. We'll talk. You might want to read them to Devon, though."

As the police escorted Devon out of the haunted house, one of them reciting his rights to him as they went, Mel, Dana, and Marco exchanged troubled glances. The tension in the air was palpable as they realized just how tangled this web had become. With every new piece of information, the mystery only seemed to grow deeper, and time was running out to find the truth before more lives were lost.

CHAPTER 13

Mel leaned against the wall, arms crossed over her broad shoulders, as she watched her wife Dana pacing back and forth on the worn carpet in front of the mismatched chairs in the waiting area of the Gatlinburg Police Station. Marco, Dana's father, sat nearby, idly flipping through an outdated magazine.

"Mel, do you think they'll listen to us?" Dana asked, stopping her pacing to glance at her wife.

"Let's hope so," Mel replied with a furrowed brow. "We need to make sure they know Devon isn't responsible for what happened to Slater."

Marco grunted in agreement, tossing the magazine onto a side table. "And we've got other suspects to consider too. Wesley being one of them."

As if on cue, the door to the station swung open and Wesley Collins strolled in, his face a mix of annoyance and worry. He didn't seem to notice Mel, Marco, and Dana as he approached the front desk.

"Crane, Rossi, Rossi-Crane," called out a uniformed officer from a nearby doorway. "They're ready for your statements."

The trio exchanged a quick glance before rising from their seats and following the officer toward the interview rooms, leaving Wesley behind in the waiting area.

"Could be our break," Marco whispered as they walked down the hallway, his eyes narrowing. "If Wesley slips up during questioning, it might lead us to the real killer."

Mel nodded, her mind racing with possibilities. What would they learn about the case? And how could they use that information to bring justice to those affected by the murders?

In the interview room, the gray walls seemed to close in around them. A plain table and a few chairs were the only furnishings. They settled into their seats, awaiting the detectives' arrival. Each carried their own suspicions and theories about the case, but they were united in their determination to uncover the truth.

As the door opened and two detectives entered the room, Mel took a deep breath, bracing herself for the questions that would follow. She knew the stakes were high and that every detail mattered.

"Good afternoon, I'm Detective Reynolds, and this is my partner, Detective Thompson," said one detective, a tall woman with a stern expression. "We'll be taking your statements about what happened tonight and anything else you three would like to share about our ongoing cases."

Mel recognized them both. The short, stocky man with graying hair, Thompson, had been the one to question Cole earlier that day.

"Sure thing, detective," Marco replied, nodding to both Reynolds and to Thompson. "Before we begin," Marco interjected, his voice firm yet steady, "I just want to clarify that Devon has been wrongly accused. He's a good man and had nothing to do with Slater's murder. I was standing right beside him the night that happened, watching him at his board, turning on all of those animatronics. First off, I don't think what he was doing shut the lights down in the haunt, and second, he never moved from his spot."

"Mr. Rossi, we understand your concern, but we're following all leads," Detective Thompson responded, his tone neutral. "If you have information that can help us determine the truth, we're more than willing to listen."

"Actually, we do have some suspicions," Dana chimed in, glancing at Mel and Marco for support. "Wesley Collins seems like he might have a motive, especially after what happened between Slater and his daughter, Renee."

"Plus, Wesley runs that haunted house attraction, and he's been acting strangely ever since we arrived in town," added Mel, recalling their earlier encounters with the enigmatic man. "It's possible he knows something that he's not telling us."

"Interesting," mused Detective Reynolds, jotting down notes on her pad. "We'll certainly keep that in mind during our investigation."

"Please remember that these are just our theories," Marco emphasized. "But we believe that exploring all possibilities is crucial in a case like this."

"Of course," Detective Thompson agreed. "Now, let's get started with your individual statements."

As the questioning began, Mel, Marco, and Dana shared everything they knew about the case, hoping that their insights would contribute to solving the mystery. They were determined to uncover the truth, not only for Slater and Elena but also for Cole whom they knew was innocent, and for Devon, whom they believed was innocent.

Despite the heaviness of their task, it seemed the more they talked, the clearer the picture became.

"By the way," Detective Reynolds said after a pause, "we've discovered that Elena Reyes had connections to Wesley's haunted house business. She was actually in charge of their financial records."

"I looked her up," Dana admitted. "She was a CPA and advertised Wesley as being a satisfied customer, so it tracks that she would handle all of his financials. It's possible that there's some other kind of financial motive behind all of this."

"Could be," Detective Thompson agreed. "We're still looking into it, but we appreciate you bringing up Wesley as a person of interest. It certainly adds another layer to the investigation."

"Speaking of persons of interest," Detective Reynolds continued, "we wanted to inform you that both Brad Marsh and Devon are now under suspicion for both murders."

"Devon? Still?" Marco asked, surprised. "I mean, I know he was there for one, but I just told you he never moved. Does he really have the ability to commit two murders? The time? Those teenagers tonight saw him somewhere else during the time Elena's murder was probably taking place. Brad too."

"Unfortunately, we can't rule anyone out at this point," Detective Thompson replied. "His purported connection to Brad and, given the sound of the exchange the two minors overheard, his interest in the local real estate market make him a viable suspect or accomplice."

"We understand your concerns," Detective Reynolds assured Marco. "However, given the complexity of this case, we need to keep all potential suspects on our radar. We're not saying Devon is guilty, but we can't ignore any possibilities."

Mel felt a knot forming in her stomach. Despite their efforts to defend Devon, it seemed like the police were determined to keep him on their list of suspects. She knew they had to find solid evidence to clear his name and ultimately bring the true killer or killers to justice.

She felt far more strongly about Brad and Wesley, than she ever felt about Devon.

"Alright," Mel said reluctantly, trying to suppress her frustration. "But, again, there's the alibi Beth and Cole provided for Devon. That has to count for something."

Detective Thompson sighed. "It does, but we're still waiting on the exact time of death determination for Elena. If it turns out his alibi, doesn't hold up, we'll be back to square one."

"Besides," Detective Reynolds added, "it's convenient for us to hold Devon for a couple of days. That way he won't be tempted to leave town while we conduct our investigation."

Mel clenched her fists, feeling anger bubble inside her at the thought of Devon being detained without solid evidence against him. She knew the detectives were just doing their jobs, but she couldn't help but feel like they were going down the wrong path.

"Fine," Mel grumbled, forcing herself to remain composed. "Just... keep an open mind, alright? There are other suspects, and I don't want Devon to be treated unfairly because you've got tunnel vision."

"Of course, Sheriff Crane," Detective Thompson said, nodding his head in understanding. "We appreciate your input and will continue the investigation with all possibilities in mind."

"Good," Mel replied, trying to mask her dissatisfaction. Internally, she vowed to pursue her own line of inquiry, focusing on those she suspected were truly behind the murders: Wesley and Brad.

As the family left the interview room, Mel's mind raced with possible scenarios and connections she needed to explore further. However, she realized that first, she had to ensure that the police didn't put all their efforts into investigating Devon.

"Detective Reynolds, before we leave this room, I want you to confirm that Cole is in the clear for Slater's murder," Mel said, her voice firm and determined. "We were told earlier today the evidence from the crime lab supports his innocence, it was prop blood on the knife and the blade was too wide to have made the lethal injury, so let's not waste any more time on him."

"Agreed, Sheriff Crane," Detective Reynolds replied. "We've reviewed the lab results, and it's clear that Cole wasn't involved in Slater's death. Our focus will be on the other suspects."

"Good," Mel nodded. "Now, let me lay out an argument for you. Consider Wesley Collins. He had more than enough motive to kill Slater."

"Go on," Detective Thompson prompted, crossing his arms over his chest.

"Think about it," Mel continued, her voice growing more passionate as she laid out her theory. "Slater was dating Wesley's daughter, Renee, but she turned down a marriage proposal, broke her heart, and drove her away. It's no secret that Wesley was furious with Slater, and he certainly had the means to set up Cole to take the fall for the murder. It's his haunted house. He assigned Cole his role and gave him that knife."

"Interesting," Detective Reynolds mused. "And Wesley would have intimate knowledge of the haunted house in the dark and access to all the lighting panels and power boxes."

"Exactly," Mel agreed. "Slater was flirting with Cole, right under Wesley's nose that night. It's possible that Wesley set Cole up to be framed, doused the lights, then killed Slater in a fit of rage, seeking vengeance for his daughter. Then he brought the house lights back up. Slater was dead on the floor and Cole was standing right there with a supposedly bloody knife."

The detectives exchanged glances, clearly considering Mel's theory. Although they said nothing, Mel could see that her words had made an impact.

"Alright, Sheriff Crane," Detective Thompson finally said. "We'll look into Wesley as well. Like I said before, we're keeping an open mind with this investigation."

"Thank you," Mel replied, feeling a bit more at ease now that the detectives seemed to take her concerns seriously.

With that, the family exited the interrogation room, their minds filled with theories and suspicions.

As they walked through the station, Dana looked around for Wesley. When she saw he wasn't around, she brought up another angle. "There's still Elena's death that needs to be explained. "We've been focusing on Slater, but we can't forget about her."

"True," Marco agreed. And that she was doing all the financial work for Wesley's haunted house business could be significant."

"Exactly," Mel chimed in. "Maybe there's something shady going on with the money, and Elena found out about it. That could be a motive for both Wesley and Meredith Marsh since one of you mentioned that there's a tie between Elena and her through bank records," she said to Thompson and Reynolds.

"Again," Reynolds said, "It could be legitimate business, but it's worth looking into."

Dana interjected, "Meredith has been trying to buy out Wesley's haunted house and everything else in that area for a while now. Maybe she was using Elena to dig up dirt on Wesley or his finances, hoping to force him to sell. Or, maybe Meredith is involved in having Elena cook the books for the haunted house and its finances," she suggested. "It would make sense that she wanted Elena out of the picture."

"Either way," Mel sighed, "we're back to Wesley and his haunted house being at the center of all this. It seems like everyone connected to this case has a reason to want him out of the picture—or worse."

"Let's not jump to conclusions," Marco cautioned. "We need solid evidence before we can accuse anyone of anything."

"Agreed," Mel replied. "But we should keep our eyes open and stay alert. We don't know who we can trust, and we have to be prepared for anything.

"Speaking of trust," Detective Ramirez interjected, "I should inform you that Meredith Marsh is currently out of town, making her unavailable for questioning. We'll have to wait until she returns to get any insight from her."

"Out of town?" Dana frowned. "That's awfully convenient, isn't it?"

"Perhaps," Ramirez conceded. "But Mr. Rossi just said, we can't make assumptions without evidence. In the meantime, we've issued an APB for Brad Marsh's arrest. Once we locate him, we can question him about his involvement with Slater and Elena."

"Good," Mel said, her jaw clenched. "The sooner we get answers, the sooner we can put this all behind us."

CHAPTER 14

It was dark outside, well after 11:00, when an exhausted Mel, Dana, and Marco finally walked out of the Gatlinburg Police Department. The tension in the air was palpable, but for a moment, they all felt a small sense of relief at leaving the stuffy station behind. Marco stretched his arms above his head, trying to ease the stiffness that had settled into his shoulders.

"Finally," he muttered under his breath, sharing a weary glance with his daughter.

Just as they reached Mel and Dana's car, however, the sudden shout of the desk sergeant stopped them in their tracks. "Sheriff Crane! Wait!" He jogged over to the three of them, his face flushed from running. "Something's come up. We need you all to come back inside."

Mel exchanged a puzzled look with her wife before nodding at the sergeant. "Alright, let's go," she said, guiding her small entourage back towards the station. They followed her lead, their steps heavy and reluctant.

"Any idea what this could be about?" Dana asked the Sargent, her voice low as they walked. Her brow furrowed with concern.

"None," he replied, shaking his head. "Reynolds said to try to get you."

"Whatever it is," Mel said, "it must be important if they're calling us back in." She glanced at Marco, catching the worry in his eyes.

As the group filed back into the waiting room, the atmosphere grew thick with anticipation. The small space seemed to close in around them, trapping them within its confines.

Mel's mind raced as she tried to decipher the reason for their sudden return to the station. She played through recent events, searching for any clue or detail that might provide an answer. But the harder she looked, the more everything seemed to blur together.

"Let's just focus on the fact we're maybe one step closer to finding the truth," Mel said quietly, hoping to reassure not only Dana and Marco but also herself.

They settled into the uncomfortable chairs once again, eyes darting between each other and the closed door that separated them from the answers they sought. As minutes drug by, the weight of uncertainty continued to press down upon them, until it became almost unbearable.

Dana decided to use the waiting time to call the hospital for an update on Jesse's condition. She fished her phone out of her pocket and dialed her mother's familiar number, her heart pounding in her chest as she waited for Chloe to pick up.

"Hey Mom, it's Dana. How's Jesse doing?" Dana asked, her voice a mixture of concern and exhaustion.

"Still no news," Chloe replied with a shaky breath. "The doctors said they'll keep us informed, but it's hard to just sit here and wait."

"Tell me about it," Dana muttered, glancing at Mel and Marco who were both visibly on edge. "We're still at the police station. They asked us to come back inside, but we don't know why yet."

"Any updates on the case?" Chloe inquired, her tone betraying her own need for a distraction from their current situation.

Dana sighed, running a hand through her hair. "Not much, but there are a couple of new leads. We told them Wesley might be involved, and there's evidence pointing towards Brad and possibly Meredith, too. They also have a fixation on Devon."

"Devon?" Chloe asked, her voice rising a few octaves in disbelief, before she reversed herself. "Well, come to think of it, he was at that wake. He certainly seems to be tied to Slater, but what about Elena?"

"No idea. It's all so confusing, Mom. And now we're back here waiting for... something. I'm not even sure what's going on anymore," Dana admitted, her frustration evident.

"Alright, honey. Just keep us updated, okay? We're all worried about Jesse and you guys too," Chloe responded, her voice filled with love and concern.

"Will do, Mom. Love you," Dana whispered, hanging up the phone. She turned to Mel and Marco, relaying the lack of news about Jesse's condition. Their expressions tightened with concern, but they nodded in understanding.

As the three of them sat in the waiting room, they couldn't help but feel as if they were on the cusp of a revelation. The air was heavy knowing that answers might be close, and yet still frustratingly out of reach.

"Mel, Marco, Dana, could you please come with us?" a uniformed officer interrupted their tense silence. The three of them exchanged glances before standing and following him into another room.

Back at the hospital, the group huddled together in the waiting room, trying to make sense of the information Dana had shared. They needed something to distract them from their concern about Jesse, and analyzing the case seemed like the best option.

"Okay, so let's go over what we know, again," Kris began, biting her lip as she thought. "Elena and Slater were killed, and there's some connection between them, Devon, Brad, and possibly Meredith."

"Right," Chloe agreed, her eyes narrowing as she tried to piece things together. "We know Devon was involved in some shady business with Brad. What if Elena found out about it, and that's why she was killed?"

"Or maybe she stumbled upon something even worse," Faye chimed in, her face pale but determined. "Something that connects all of them somehow."

"Let's not jump to conclusions," Chloe cautioned, her years of being a cop's wife reminding them all to stay grounded. "We need to focus on the facts and try to find the connections between the victims and the suspects."

The family members nodded and began discussing the possible motives and connections between everyone involved. As they bounced theories off each other, their minds raced through the tangled web of relationships and events that had led them to this point. Their voices overlapped as they passionately debated the evidence, each one offering new perspectives and insights.

"Could somebody have been jealous? Maybe one of them felt jealous of another one," Cole suggested, looking from one family member to another for input.

"Or money," Lance added. "There's usually a financial motive somewhere."

"Whatever it is, we need to find the truth," Hannah said resolutely, her eyes filled with fierce determination.

As the discussion continued, each family member clung to their theories, desperate to make sense of the nightmare they found themselves in on what was supposed to be a relaxing vacation.

Faye, her arms crossed defensively over her chest, spoke up. "I still think it's Brad," she said, her voice firm with conviction. "He had the means and opportunity, not to mention the motive. He was jealous of Slater, and killing her would have been his twisted way of getting back at her."

Chloe nodded in agreement. "Yes, he's definitely a prime suspect. Besides jealousy, let's not forget that he could've been doing his mother's bidding. Meredith might have wanted to get rid of Slater to discredit Wesley, and Brad would do anything to please her."

"True," Faye conceded. "And with both women, there's also the possibility of a financial kickback from Devon. We don't know the full extent of their relationship, but like Lance said, money can be a powerful motivator for murder."

As they continued discussing the case, they found themselves unable to shake the nagging feeling that Brad was indeed the killer. Despite Dana's mention of Wesley as another potential suspect, it seemed that all roads led back to Brad.

"Let's look at the facts," Chloe said, trying to maintain logic amidst the tangle of emotions swirling around the room. "Brad was Slater's ex-boyfriend. She left him like she left Renee, and then flirted with Cole in front of him, which could've triggered his jealousy. Plus, we know Devon had financial or some sort of dealings with him trying to get to his mother. It's all too much of a coincidence."

"Right," Faye chimed in. "And if Wesley were really involved, why would he risk everything by hosting this convention and bringing so much attention to himself and his haunted house? That makes little sense for him to do."

The group fell silent, each one processing the information and grappling with the heavy implications.

"Okay," Lance began, attempting to steer the conversation back on track. "Let's not forget about Elena Reyes, the other victim. We need to figure out if her murder is connected to Slater's or if it's a separate case entirely."

"From what we know, Elena was an accountant, a CPA," Lance said thoughtfully. "She could have uncovered some sort of financial misdeeds involving Devon with the Haunted House, or even with Meredith. She might have worked with Meredith too from what Dana told us. Maybe she was killed to prevent her from talking."

"Or maybe she found out something about the haunted house," Kris suggested, her eyes lighting up with the hint of a theory. "Wesley's business could have been involved in something shady."

"True," Chloe nodded. "We can't rule out Wesley completely. He had motive too, especially if Slater was causing him trouble with his haunted house venture."

As the family members continued to bounce theories off each other, they pored over the details, speculating about motives and potential connections between the victims and suspects. Each new piece of information seemed to reveal another layer of complexity, making it more challenging to untangle the web of deceit and uncover the truth.

The tension in the room rose as each family member advocated for their own theory. Faye, frowning, stated, "I maintain Brad is our top suspect." He was jealous of Slater and couldn't handle her moving on."

"Maybe," Lance conceded. "But where does Elena fit? In my mind, Wesley had just as much motive as Brad, especially if Slater was causing problems for his haunted house business. We can't ignore that, and we can't rule out Devon either. He's an electronics and animatronics expert. Who knows what secrets he could be hiding? And with his connections to the haunted house, there might be more to his involvement than we realize."

As the discussion intensified, they delved even deeper into the motives and relationships of the suspects, trying to uncover the truth behind the murders. Faye carefully studied the faces of her family members, noting their expressions of determination, fear, and uncertainty.

"Let's go back to the evidence for a moment," Chloe suggested, her voice cutting through the cacophony of theories. "We need to focus on what we know for sure and eliminate any speculation that doesn't align with the facts."

"Alright," Faye agreed, taking a deep breath to steady herself. "Let's lay out the key points we have so far: Slater and Elena were both murdered, with similar methods...opportunity. Brad had an obvious motive for killing Slater, but it's unclear why he would target Elena, unless she discovered something incriminating about him. Wesley and Devon also have potential motives, though less obvious ones."

Lance said, "We need to determine which suspect's motive makes the most sense, given the available evidence."

The family members fell silent for a moment, each lost in their thoughts as they considered the puzzle before them. It was a daunting task, but they were determined to find the answers, not only for the sake of justice but for their own peace of mind.

"Let's keep digging," Kris said resolutely, her eyes filled with resolve. "We'll find the truth, and we'll make sure the person responsible pays for what they've done."

CHAPTER 15

Dana, Mel, and Marco continued to sit on hard plastic chairs bolted to the floor in the police station lobby, their hands fidgeting nervously in their laps as they exchanged anxious glances. Mel's mind raced with all the possible outcomes of the case, her instincts as a sheriff honed to razor sharpness by years on the force. Beside her, Dana bounced in her seat as she tried to suppress her urge to pace and Marco, on the other side of Dana, leaned forward and to his right, trying to stretch his back muscles.

"Why isn't there any news yet?" Marco asked, his voice cracking under the strain.

Mel spread her hands in a gesture of defeat. "I wish I knew."

As if on cue, the double doors of the station swung open, and a group of patrol officers strode in, escorting an older man between them. The handcuffs around his wrists clinked loudly as he was led past the trio on the bench. It was Wesley Collins, his face twisted into a snarl of anger and defiance. His eyes met Mel's for a moment, sparking with an unspoken fury before he was ushered into an interrogation room.

"Isn't that--" Dana began, but Mel cut her off.

"Yep," she said grimly. "Wesley Collins. Looks like they caught him trying to burn down his own haunted house."

"How can you tell?"

Mel waved a hand in front of her nose. "Couldn't you smell him?"

"Jesus," Marco muttered, rubbing his temples. "What the hell is going on?"

"Whatever it is," Mel said, steeling herself for the task ahead, "we're about to find out."

As Wesley disappeared behind the closed door, a flurry of activity erupted throughout the station. Officers rushed back and forth, discussing the situation in hushed voices. The tension in the air crackled like electricity, charged with anticipation as conclusions loomed close.

"Mel," Dana said softly, her eyes filled with concern. "What do you think will happen next?"

"Right now, they'll question Wesley and try to piece together the evidence," Mel replied, her voice steady despite the turmoil raging inside her. "If they can connect him to the murders of Slater and Elena, we might finally get some answers."

"Let's hope so," Marco sighed, his fingers tightening around the brim of the Steelers ball cap he held in his hand. "We need to put this nightmare to rest once and for all."

The trio sat in silence, watching as the police station buzzed with activity around them. As they listened to the muffled sounds of questioning behind the closed door, each one knew that the battle for justice was far from over.

The acrid smell of smoke wafted through the air again as more people came in. Mel, Dana, and Marco huddled together in the corner of the now crowded station house. The room buzzed with frenetic energy; officers in plain clothes hurriedly relayed information to their uniformed counterparts. A cacophony of ringing phones, urgent voices, and the distant wail of sirens filled the space.

"Sounds like they finally got a handle on the fire at the haunted house," Marco muttered, his eyes never leaving the door through which Wesley had been escorted several minutes before.

"Let's hope," Mel mumbled. Her mind raced, analyzing every detail of the case. She knew she had to act quickly, before any vital evidence was lost in the chaos.

"Excuse me," she called out, catching the attention of a nearby detective. "I have some information that may help your investigation."

The detective, a tall man with graying hair, nodded curtly and approached Mel. "What do you have for us, Sheriff Crane?"

"Based on my observations, I believe Wesley's actions tonight are directly connected to the murders of Slater and Elena," Mel stated firmly, her voice steady despite the surrounding tumult.

"Go on," the detective urged, his eyes narrowing with interest.

"Both victims were involved in the haunted house business - Slater as a former employee an attendee at a walk through demonstration, and Elena as an accountant. It's possible that Wesley saw them as threats to his own venture. There are financial considerations in several ways with Elena Reyes. Make sure you check his financial records," Mel added. "Elena would have had access to sensitive information that Wesley might have wanted to keep hidden. Detectives Thompson and Reynolds can tell you more, if their reports aren't finished yet. It's only been a couple of hours since we discussed these things with them." She pointed behind her at Dana and Marco.

The detective's expression grew serious as he considered Mel's words. "That's a solid theory, Sheriff. We'll definitely look into it. Thank you," the detective said before disappearing into the sea of - officers.

Mel glanced at Dana and Marco, who both nodded in approval of her efforts. As they continued to watch the whirlwind of activity around them, Mel's thoughts raced, piecing together the fragments of the case like a jigsaw puzzle.

Twenty minutes later, Mel leaned against a wall, arms folded across her chest, her eyes fixed on the detective she'd spoken to who was now speaking to a uniformed officer.

"Get search warrants for Wesley Collins' vehicles, home, and whatever is left of his business," the detective ordered, his voice low but firm. "We need to move quickly on this."

"Understood, sir," the officer replied, hurrying away to carry out the orders.

Mel's mind raced as she pondered the implications of the search warrants. If they found evidence linking Wesley to the murders of Slater and Elena, it would be a significant breakthrough in the case. She glanced at Dana and Marco, who stood nearby, their faces etched with concern.

"Once they get those warrants, I have a feeling things will fall into place," Mel said.

"Let's hope so," Dana agreed, rubbing her hands together nervously.

"Hey, Sheriff!" a patrol officer called out, rushing towards them. "You might want in on this. We just found Brad Marsh squatting in an old cabin in McCookville, between here and Pigeon Forge."

"Brad? Found?" Mel asked, her eyebrows shooting up in surprise.

"Looks like he's been hiding out," the officer replied, catching his breath. "We've brought him in for questioning."

"Can you show me?" Mel asked, pushing herself off the wall and following the officer down the hallway without waiting for an answer.

As they entered the small interrogation room, Mel spotted Brad slumped in a chair, his hands cuffed behind his back. His face was pale and drawn, his eyes darting around the room as if seeking an escape.

"Brad, what were you thinking?" Mel asked gently, trying not to let her frustration seep into her voice. "You knew they'd find you, eventually."

"I didn't do it," Brad insisted, his voice cracking. "I'm not a killer."

"Then why were you hiding?" Marco chimed in, stepping into the room behind Mel. "If you're innocent, you have nothing to fear."

"Everyone thinks I killed Slater!" Brad exclaimed, his eyes filling with tears. "And now Elena's dead too. I didn't want to be next."

"Brad, if you know anything that can help them catch the real killer, you need to tell us, or tell the police here," Mel urged, her eyes searching his face for any sign of deception.

"I swear, I don't know anything," Brad replied, his voice barely above a whisper.

"Alright," Mel said, placing a comforting hand on his shoulder. "We'll make sure they do everything they can to keep you safe, but you need to tell them everything you know."

As Mel left the interrogation room, she hoped they were one step closer to unraveling the twisted web of lies and secrets surrounding the murders. With the search warrants in hand for the Gatlinburg PD, the truth might soon be revealed. And for the sake of everyone involved, she prayed it wouldn't be too late.

The station continued to hum with manic energy, the air thick with anticipation and determination. Officers moved about, sharing information as the detectives on duty prepared for the interrogations of both Wesley Collins and Brad Marsh. The scent of fresh coffee mingled with the faint odor of ink and paper giving the small station an almost cozy atmosphere despite the grave matters at hand.

Mel was back to leaning against a wall, her eyes focused on the flurry of activity. She had seen it countless times before in her own department, but there she had never been so personally invested in a case. Dana stood beside her, gripping her arm with a mix of support and unease. Marco observed the scene with the keen eye of a retired police lieutenant.

"God, I hope they find something," Mel muttered under her breath, her jaw clenched tight. "We need to nail this bastard."

"Mel, they know what they're doing," Dana assured her gently, rubbing her arm. "They'll find the evidence they need to get him."

Marco nodded in agreement. "Patience, Mel. You know how this all works."

As detectives filed into the separate interrogation rooms, Mel, Dana, and Marco slipped into the observation room, their gazes fixed on the one-way mirrors. Mel's heart raced in her chest, each beat a silent plea for justice.

"Alright, Mr. Collins," began the detective handling Wesley's interrogation. "We believe you were involved in the deaths of Slater Walker and Elena Reyes. Why don't you start by telling us where you were on the nights of their murders?"

"Are you kidding me?" Wesley scoffed, his expression twisted with indignation. "I was at my haunted house, working! There were more than a dozen people that were right there with me when Slater was killed. I've got nothing to do with those girls' deaths."

"Interesting," said the detective, unimpressed. "Because we found evidence linking you to the crime scenes."

"Mel, you think they really found something?" Dana whispered, her eyes wide with hope.

"Let's hope so," Mel replied, her knuckles white as she clenched her fists.

Meanwhile, in the other interrogation room, a different detective questioned Brad. "So, Mr. Marsh, can you explain why you were hiding in that abandoned cabin?"

"Everyone thinks I killed Slater!" Brad cried out, his voice cracking. "You guys. Those people out there that aren't from here, and then I went into my house and saw Elena...I was scared!"

"Scared of what, exactly?" the detective pressed.

"Of being accused! Of...of whoever really did it coming after me next!" Brad stammered, his eyes filling with tears.

"Or maybe you feared getting caught?" the detective suggested, his tone skeptical.

"Dammit, I didn't do it!" Brad insisted, slamming his hands on the table.

Mel's brow furrowed as she watched both interrogations unfold. Her instincts screamed Wesley was involved, but she couldn't shake the nagging feeling that there was more to the story. She glanced at Dana and Marco, their expressions a mix of concern and determination.

"Something isn't adding up," Mel murmured, her eyes never leaving the one-way mirror. "We need to find the missing piece."

"Then let's help them, if they'll let us," Marco urged. "We know how to sift through stuff just as well as they do. They need extra experienced hands. We can help them figure this out."

"Right," agreed Dana, her grip on Mel's arm tightening. "We'll help put an end to this nightmare, once and for all."

The fluorescent lighting overhead flickered and hummed, bathing the documents and photographs strewn across the table in a harsh white light. Mel peered closely at the items before her, her forehead wrinkled in thought. Dana and Marco stood nearby, tensely watching Mel's examination of the evidence.

"Look at this," Mel said, pointing to a paper printed photograph of burned debris from Wesley's haunted house. "The fire was started deliberately; he piled stuff up in the middle of the floor and lit it. It's not just an accident."

"Right," Dana agreed, her eyes scanning the image. "So, either he was just that angry at it all or he was trying to destroy any evidence linking him to Slater's and Elena's deaths."

"Exactly," Mel nodded, her mind racing. "But what exactly is he hiding?"

As if on cue, an officer entered the room with a stack of documents in hand. "We've got a start getting Wesley's financial records," he announced, placing them on the table. "Maybe there's something here that can help us. All the detectives are tied up, so we could sure use some extra hands...since you're already here and helping."

"Let's see," Marco muttered. He started looking through the papers slowly, then began rifling through them with growing interest.

"There are several payments made to 'Brad Marsh.' Why would Wesley pay Brad?"

"Hmm. Maybe he was paying him off," Mel suggested, her gaze sharpening. "To keep quiet about something he knew?"

"Or maybe they were in it all together," Dana added, her voice low and urgent.

"Either way, we have a connection," Mel said firmly. "Now we need to find out why."

"Wait," Marco whispered, his eyes widening as he pointed to another document. "This is a property deed for land in McCookville, which is where that officer said the abandoned cabin is where Brad was found. And guess whose name is on it?"

"Wesley Collins," Mel breathed, as she looked over at the deed. "He owns that land. That's motive: He could be framing Brad to cover up his own involvement."

"Or they were working together," Dana suggested, "And something went wrong."

"Whatever it is," Mel said, her voice steely with determination. "We're onto them now."

Together, the trio delved deeper into the tangled web of Wesley's finances and connections, their resolve only growing stronger as the evidence mounted against him. As Mel's keen instincts and Dana and Marco's attention to detail guided their investigation, it became increasingly clear that they were on the verge of uncovering the truth.

"Let's take this to the detectives," Mel said as she gathered gathering the incriminating documents in a neat stack. "It's time to confront Wesley with what we've found."

As they watched through the mirror, in one corner of the interrogation room a uniformed officer tapped his foot impatiently, his hand resting on his holstered gun as he waited for instructions. The atmosphere in the observation room was charged with anticipation, each person present acutely aware that they were on the cusp of solving a gruesome double homicide.

"Mel," Dana whispered, her voice barely audible over the hum of activity. "I can't believe we're this close to pinning it on Wesley."

"Neither can I," Mel admitted, wiping her sweaty palms on her jeans. "But we still need to be cautious. We don't know what he's capable of."

As if on cue, the door to the interrogation room swung open and a detective entered, his face a mask of grim determination. He strode towards them, clutching a sheaf of papers in one hand.

"I'm Detective Lucius. Night shift. We're going to confront Wesley now for everything we've collectively found. If there's anything else you haven't already given me you can add to the evidence Thompson, Reynolds, and I have collected as we go along, speak up."

"Understood," Mel said, exchanging a glance with Dana and Marco.

As the detective led them into the room, an icy chill seemed to settle over Mel. She knew that whatever happened next, there was no turning back. And yet, as she squared her shoulders and met the gazes of her wife and her father-in-law, she found herself filled with a fierce determination to see justice done.

"Ready?" the detective asked, his hand resting on the door handle.

"Ready," Mel confirmed, her voice steady and resolute.

"Let's do this," Dana added, her eyes flashing with resolve.

"Right behind you," Marco agreed, his expression one of grim determination.

The detective nodded, pulling the door open and stepping inside. As Mel followed him into the room, steeling herself for the confrontation ahead, she knew that they had done everything in their power to build a case against Wesley Collins. Now, it was time to make sure he answered for his crimes.

CHAPTER 16

They didn't get far. Before the door to the interrogation room closed, an officer hurried in and whispered something to the detective.

The detective stood and waved them all back out of the room. "There's been a fresh development." To Wesley Collins, he said, "Sit tight."

In the lobby stood a furious Meredith Marsh. Her usually immaculate appearance was marred by hastily combed hair and a rumpled business suit. She radiated indignation like a high-voltage power line.

"Can someone explain to me why I was dragged out of bed at this ungodly hour?" she demanded, glaring daggers at the officers who had escorted her in.

"Sorry, ma'am," one of them mumbled, unease written across his face. "We were instructed to bring you in for questioning immediately."

"Questioning? About what? I just got back from a business trip!" She crossed her arms in defiance.

"Mrs. Marsh, please calm down," Detective Lucius said firmly, stepping forward. "We have some important questions to ask you, and we'd appreciate your cooperation."

"Fine." Meredith huffed, her nostrils flaring. "But I expect an explanation."

"Of course," he assured her, gesturing to the only interrogation room that was empty. "Let's talk privately, and we can clear up any confusion." Lucius nodded toward Mel and directed her to the room as well.

As they led Meredith away, Marco raised an eyebrow at his daughter, Dana. "Well, that's certainly an interesting development."

"Isn't it?" Dana replied, her gaze shifting between the two interrogation rooms. "Now we just need to figure out how she fits into all this."

"Let's hope Lucius and Mel can get some answers," Marco said, his eyes narrowing as they walked toward the observation room again so they could watch Meredith's questioning unfold.

"Mel will get it done," Dana stated confidently, watching her wife take a seat next to Detective Lucius, across from Meredith, who seemed to do her best to maintain an air of superiority despite the circumstances.

"Alright, let's start with your early return from your business trip," Lucius began.

"Fine, yes. I came back early because I had finished my meetings, and I wanted to surprise my son," Meredith admitted begrudgingly, her eyes darting around the room as if searching for an escape route.

"Interesting," Mel mused, taking note of Meredith's evasiveness. "And you were completely unaware of what transpired at your home during your absence?"

"Of course not!" Meredith snapped, her hands clenched tightly in her lap. "I would never condone something like that!"

Mel raised an eyebrow. "Condone? Interesting choice of word. What do you think happened in your home?"

"I'm assuming some sort of party that got out of hand. I'm always telling Brad—"

"Let's cut to the chase, Mrs. Marsh," Detective Lucius said gruffly. "Do you know where your son Brad is?"

"Of course not!" Meredith retorted, her voice quivering slightly. "I just got home last night. I haven't seen him since I left for my trip."

"Interesting," Lucius replied, his eyes narrowing. He slid a set of photographs across the table toward Meredith. "These were taken at your residence. Elena Reyes was found murdered there."

Meredith paled, her breath catching in her throat as she stared down at the grisly images. "No...no, this can't be real."

"Unfortunately, it is," Mel chimed in, her voice cold. "Did you see or hear anything when you arrived home last night?"

"It was late, dark. I was exhausted. I noticed nothing amiss," Meredith admitted, her voice barely above a whisper. "I just went straight to bed."

"Would you mind telling us about your relationship with Elena?" Lucius asked, watching Meredith carefully.

"Like I told you before, she used to work for me," Meredith snapped, suddenly defensive. "That's all."

"No. First time I'm hearing it," Lucius said. "Worked, or was still working?"

"Used to," Meredith ground out. "She's a CPA, but only part time in this area. She lived half the year in godforsaken Ohio. I need full-time financial people in my business."

"When did Elena stop working for you, Ms. Marsh?"

"Mrs. I'm a widow in mourning. I still use Mrs."

Stay on her, Mel thought.

"Fine. "When did Elena stop working for you, Mrs. Marsh?"

"Look, I don't know what you're trying to insinuate, but I had nothing to do with any of this," Meredith insisted, her eyes shining with unshed tears. "I just want to find my son and make sure he's okay!"

"Trust me, Mrs. Marsh, we want to find Brad too," Detective Lucius assured her, knowing all the while Brad was in the interrogation room next door, between her and Wesley Collins. "But we need your cooperation if we're going to get to the bottom of this."

"Fine," Meredith said, her voice strained. "Ask your questions."

As Mel and Detective Lucius continued to probe Meredith for information, Dana and Marco watched from behind the one-way glass, their faces grim.

"Something's not adding up here," Marco muttered, his eyes never leaving Meredith's face.

"Agreed," Dana replied, her brow furrowed in concern. "But what is she hiding?" They watched as Detective Lucius leaned in, his eyes never leaving Meredith's. "Mrs. Marsh, we understand you had an interest in acquiring Mr. Collins' haunted house property. Is that correct?"

Meredith hesitated for a moment before replying, "Yes, that's true. It's prime real estate, and I had plans to develop it into something more profitable."

"Like what?" Mel interjected, her voice calm but firm.

"Condos, shops, maybe even a grand hotel right there on the Parkway," Meredith answered, a hint of irritation creeping into her tone. "Does that really matter?"

"Actually, it does," Detective Lucius said. "You see, Mrs. Marsh, we believe you had ulterior motives for wanting that property so badly. And we think Elena was involved in your scheme."

Meredith's eyes widened, and she shook her head vigorously. "No, you've got it all wrong!"

"Then explain this," Mel said, sliding a financial document across the table. "It shows that you paid Elena a considerable sum of money to cook Wesley's books, making it look like he was losing money on his haunted house. Why would you want him to believe his business was failing if not to persuade him to sell the property to you for a fraction of its worth?"

The blood drained from Meredith's face, and she stared at the paper as if it were a venomous snake. "I... I didn't want anyone to get hurt. I just wanted that property. It was the last piece of the puzzle for my development plans."

"By manipulating Elena and putting her in danger," Mel stated coldly. "And now she's dead, along with Slater Walker."

"Look, I never meant for any of this to happen," Meredith cried, tears streaming down her face. "I just wanted to secure my family's future. Please, you have to believe me!"

As Mel and Detective Lucius exchanged a knowing glance, Dana leaned toward Marco behind the one-way glass. "She's hiding something more," she whispered. "I can feel it."

Mel left the observation room and strode down the hallway, her mind racing with the revelations from Meredith's interrogation. As she approached the waiting area, she spotted Brad Marsh now sitting out there on a hard plastic chair, his legs bouncing nervously.

"Brad," Mel called out, capturing his attention. "Come with me."

"Is my mom okay?" he asked as they walked toward an empty interview room. "An officer told me she's here."

"Your mother has been picked up and is being questioned about some things," Mel explained. She motioned for him to sit down at the table and took a seat across from him. "Now, I need you to be honest with me. What do you know about Slater's murder?"

Brad swallowed hard, his eyes darting around the room. "I-I don't know anything about that. I loved her once, but she didn't feel the same."

"Brad, we know you were involved in helping Devon with something," Mel pressed, her voice firm. "Tell me what you did and why."

His answer surprised her. He hesitated, then sighed, his shoulders slumping. "Devon offered me money to help him rig some animatronics for Wesley's haunted house. I didn't ask questions; I just did as I was told. But I never wanted anyone to get hurt."

"Did you know your mother paid Elena to manipulate Wesley's finances?" Mel asked, her gaze unwavering despite his revelation.

"Wh-what? No!" Brad exclaimed, genuine surprise written across his face. "I had no idea. My mom... she can be ruthless when it comes to business, but I never thought she'd go that far."

"Unfortunately, she did," Mel confirmed. "And now two people are dead because of it."

Back in the observation room, Dana and Marco watched as Mel and Detective Lucius entered the room where Wesley Collins sat defiantly, his hands cuffed to the table.

"Mr. Collins," Mel began, placing a folder on the table in front of him. "We have some new information regarding your haunted house and the murders of Slater Walker and Elena Reyes."

Wesley scoffed, his eyes narrowing. "I've already told you everything I know."

"Your daughter's former girlfriend's ex-boyfriend, Brad Marsh, has admitted to helping Devon rig the animatronics in your haunted house," Lucius revealed, his tone icy. "And we have evidence that Meredith Marsh paid Elena to cook your books, making it look like you were losing money on the business."

"Meridith and Elena wanted me out so they could buy my property for cheap," Wesley spat, his face growing red. "But I never laid a finger on either of those women!"

"Then how do you explain these?" Mel demanded, pulling out photographs of the piles of burned out props and animatronics at the haunted house.

As Wesley stared at the images, his confidence faltered. He glanced at Detective Lucius, who loomed over him with an unyielding expression, before looking back at Mel. For the first time since they'd met, there was a flicker of fear in his eyes.

"Tell us the truth, Collins," Mel urged, her voice laced with determination. "It's only a matter of time before the arson squad from Knoxville goes digging through all of that and uncovers what you were trying to destroy."

Wesley's eyes darted around the room, his breathing growing shallow as he realized the walls were closing in on him. He clenched his fists under the table and swallowed hard, trying to regain his composure.

"Fine," he growled. "Maybe I helped Brad and Devon rig the animatronics, but it was only to protect my business. They came to me with their plan to save it and make it a destination haunt for Devon's work, and I had no choice."

Mel leaned in closer, her gaze unrelenting. "But that doesn't explain the murders. Did you kill Slater and Elena to keep them quiet and frame Brad Marsh for their deaths?"

"Of course not!" Wesley exclaimed, slamming his fist against the table. "I would never hurt anyone!"

"Yet, Slater was killed inside your haunted house during a walk through arranged and led by you, and there is evidence that you sent a text to Elena Reyes asking to meet up at Meredith's house yesterday, where she died," Mel said calmly, raising an eyebrow. "The PD has her phone. Coincidence? I think not."

Wesley hesitated, his mouth opening and closing several times before finally speaking. "Alright... I didn't mean to kill Slater. It was an accident. She discovered our plan and threatened to expose us to Meridith out of spite because of our history. Meridith would have cut Brad out of everything. I tried a couple of things to scare her off, but she was a defiant, do as she damn well pleases sort of person. She showed up at the walkthrough and things...well, they got out of hand."

"And what about Elena?" Mel pressed, her voice steady and unwavering.

"Devon killed her," Wesley whispered, his shoulders slumping in defeat. "He thought she was onto our scheme and she was going to rat us out after Slater's death. I didn't want him to, but he insisted it was the only way to save our skins. He was trying to frame Meredith, not Brad."

As Wesley's confession hung in the air, a heavy silence fell over the interrogation room. Mel glanced at Detective Lucius, who gave her a curt nod, acknowledging their success.

Dana and Marco watched through the one-way glass, still not sure they had the full truth. Devon had an established alibi that would have to be disproven. She was finally thankful Devon was in holding after all. He, Wesley, and Brad could rat each other out.

"Mr. Collins," Detective Lucius said, "you're under arrest for the murders of Slater Walker and Elena Reyes. You have the right to remain silent. Anything you say can and will be used against you in a court of law."

As Wesley hung his head, the weight of his guilt finally settling upon him, Mel knew that justice was being served. But her father was ailing, and there were still more mysteries to unravel and more criminals to apprehend back home, and she couldn't afford to waste any more time.

CHAPTER 17

The hospital waiting room was a suffocating mix of stale air, anxiety, and hushed voices as the Crane and Rossi families clustered together, their expressions mirroring one another's concern. The tension in the room was palpable, like a thread stretched taut between them all.

Mel sat in a generic waiting room armchair with her back to the wall, her tall, broad-shouldered frame tense despite her attempt at maintaining a stoic demeanor. Dana sat beside her, fingers fidgeting with a tissue that had long since been reduced to shreds. Mel caught herself staring at the door for the hundredth time, willing it to open and reveal the doctor with news about her father.

"Any minute now," Marco muttered, his voice tight. He was pacing the length of the small waiting area much as his daughter had done at the police station, the restless energy of a retired police lieutenant still evident in his stride. His wife Chloe, usually an animated conversationalist, sat quietly by his side, her eyes fixed on her hands folded neatly in her lap.

"Grandpa's strong, right?" Cole asked Mel, seeking reassurance from his aunt. His face, often a youthful picture of confidence, when he wasn't being accused of murder, was now etched with worry.

"He's a fighter," Mel replied, trying to sound more convinced than she felt. "He'll pull through this."

"Mom's gonna be so upset if something happens to him," Beth whispered, her voice barely audible. "Grandma, too." She gnawed on her lower lip, her leg bouncing nervously.

Faye Crane took all their words in, then leaned forward, her eyes closed. Her lips moved silently as she prayed for her husband's recovery. It struck Mel how small and frail Faye looked in that moment, her usual strength replaced by a vulnerability that tugged at Mel's heart.

"Jesse has always faced challenges head-on," Marco said into the silence, stopping his pacing to stand between Faye and Chloe. "This is just another one of those challenges."

"Right," Chloe agreed, her voice shaky but determined. "And we'll all be here to support him, won't we?"

As the family exchanged nods of agreement, Mel couldn't help but wonder if their collective resolve would be enough to carry them through the trials ahead. The door remained closed, and the waiting continued, each second ticking by like an eternity.

When the door to the waiting room finally swung open an hour later, a middle-aged doctor in a white coat strode in. The families' collective breath caught in their throats as they watched him approach, their hearts pounding in unison. Mel's fingers unconsciously tightened around Faye's hand.

"Mr. Crane's family?" The doctor asked, his voice steady, but not without warmth.

"That's all of us here," Mel replied, her voice wavering only slightly. "This is my mother Faye, his wife," she told the man as she held up

Faye's hand she had clasped in her own. She braced herself for the news.

"Jesse's stents are working well," the doctor announced, his eyes meeting Mel's and then Faye's. "Assuming he continues to progress as expected, we'll be able to release him later today."

A flood of relief washed over the room, as though someone had thrown wide a window to let in fresh air. Smiles blossomed on faces that had been taut with worry just moments before. Mel felt tears prick at the corners of her eyes, while Faye openly wept, her shoulders shaking with emotion.

"Thank you, Doctor," Marco said, stepping forward to grasp the man's hand in a firm shake. "We're all so grateful."

"Thank you very much," Chloe echoed, wiping tears from her cheeks with one hand while she gently squeezed the doctor's arm with the other.

"Your husband is a strong man," the doctor said to Faye, who was still too choked up to speak. "He has a lot to live for, and that's an incredible motivator." "Indeed, it is," Faye whispered, her voice thick with emotion.

"Can we see him now?" Mel asked, trying to maintain her composure as she fought back her own tears.

"Of course," the doctor replied, gesturing towards the door. "I'll have the nurse show you to his room. No more than two at a time though and keep it short. Remember, he needs rest and support to ensure a full recovery."

"Rest and support?" Mel echoed, a smile playing at the corners of her mouth. "I think we can handle that."

The family exchanged hugs and words of thanks, their relief palpable in the air.

As she and Faye followed the nurse down the hallway towards Jesse's room, Mel couldn't help but marvel at the power of love and determination. They had come together as one, united in their concern for Jesse, and now they would face his recovery with the same unwavering resolve.

"Here's to new beginnings," she murmured, her voice barely audible over the hum of medical equipment and the quiet conversations around her.

As Mel and Faye entered Jesse's hospital room, they found him propped up in bed, his face pale but animated as he chatted with the attending nurse. The steady beeping of the heart monitor punctuated their conversation, a constant reminder of the fragility of life.

"Hey, you two," Jesse said, breaking into a grin when he saw them. "Come on in."

Faye rushed to his side, her hands trembling ever so slightly as she reached out to touch his cheek. "Jesse... I'm so thankful you're alright."

"Me too," he replied, his voice warm and sincere, devoid of its usual gruffness, as he took her hand. "I couldn't have gotten through this without you and Mel."

"Of course, Dad," Mel said, joining them at the bedside. "We're family, after all."

"I know," Jesse said, his eyes shining with unshed tears. "But it still means the world to me."

"Let's focus on getting you better, Dad," Mel insisted, her gaze never leaving his face.

"Absolutely," Jesse agreed, his tone resolute. "I've got a whole list of medications I'll need to take now, and the doctor says I'll need to make some pretty significant changes to my diet and exercise routine...gotta start exercising, but I want to do everything in my power to prevent another scare like this."

"Good," Faye said, nodding her approval. "We'll help you every step of the way."

"Thanks, you two," Jesse murmured, his voice cracking with emotion. "I don't know what I'd do without you."

"Same here, Dad," Mel replied, squeezing his hand. "You're not going anywhere."

"Damn right," Jesse chuckled, his eyes twinkling with determination. "I've got too much living left to do."

"Alright then," Mel said, clapping her hands together. "Let's get to work."

After a round of gentle laughter, Mel shared a quiet moment with her father, her heart swelling with pride and gratitude as she watched him face his recovery head-on, then she left to get Kris and send her in for a turn with him.

Hours later, the sterile smell of the hospital waiting room hung in the air as Mel stood by the window, her eyes tracing the path that the ambulance would probably take to take her father back to Ohio. She could feel the weight of responsibility settling on her shoulders, knowing that she and Faye would be the ones to ensure Jesse's successful recovery.

"Once we get him home, we'll need to set up a schedule for his medications and make sure he follows the doctor's orders," Mel said, her voice firm with determination.

Faye nodded, looking equally resolute. "I'll start researching heart-healthy recipes and look into finding a nutritionist. Exercise will be crucial too. Maybe we can all go for daily walks together."

"Good idea," Mel agreed, appreciating Faye's proactive approach. "We'll need to keep a close eye on him, especially in the beginning. He's stubborn, but I think this scare has made him realize he needs to change."

"You're right," Faye replied, her hand reaching for Mel's. "We'll do it together, like we always have."

As they spoke, the rest of the Crane and Rossi families gathered around them, discussing the logistics of transporting Jesse back to Morelville. Marco and Chloe had already contacted the insurance company to coordinate an ambulance, while Kris and Lance were making arrangements with family friends back home to pick up prescriptions and medical supplies.

"Aunt Mel, you'll ride with Grandpa in the ambulance, right?" Cole asked, his concern for his grandfather clear in his voice.

"Of course," Mel reassured him, offering a small smile. "I wouldn't leave his side."

"Thanks, Aunt Mel," Beth chimed in. "We'll help at the farm more while he gets better. Everything will be taken care of."

"Thank you both," Mel said gratefully, her heart warmed by their support.

As the family continued to make plans, Mel's thoughts raced ahead to the challenges that awaited them. She knew that adjusting to a new lifestyle would be difficult for her dad, but she was determined to help him every step of the way.

"Alright, everyone," Marco announced, clapping his hands together. "Let's get everything in order. We have a long trip back ahead, and a long road after that, so let's get on it."

"Here's to a healthy future," Chloe added, raising an imaginary glass in toast.

"Cheers to that," Mel murmured, her eyes meeting Faye's as they shared a moment of quiet resolve.

They bustled around Jesse's hospital room and the waiting room down the hall, gathering their belongings as they prepared to leave.

The sterile white walls seemed to close in on them, but the atmosphere was filled with a quiet optimism.

"Alright, Dad," Kris began, "We're gonna head back to the cabin and get some sleep. We'll hit the road home tomorrow, a day earlier than planned."

"Sounds good," Jesse replied, his voice still weak but determined. Can't wait until we're all back in Ohio."

"Take care, Grandpa," Cole said, leaning down to embrace his grandfather gently. "You'll beat us back there, but we'll come see you and do the chores as soon as we get back."

"Please do," Jesse murmured, his eyes shining with gratitude. "I'm gonna need all the help I can get."

"Grandpa," Beth added, her voice choked with emotion, "we love you so much. You got this and we'll be right there with you."

"Thank you, sweetheart," Jesse whispered, squeezing her hand.

Mel watched the exchange from the doorway, her heart swelling with pride at her family's resilience.

"Alright, let's get you going, Mr. Crane," a nurse announced, entering the room with a wheelchair. She deftly helped Jesse into the chair, adjusting the blankets around him for comfort.

"Ready, Mom?" Mel asked, turning to Faye who was carefully packing away the last of their things.

"Of course," Faye replied, determination etched across her face. "Let's get our man home."

"Love you, Dad," Mel whispered, her hand resting on his shoulder as they made their way to the ambulance waiting outside.

"Love you too, Mel," Jesse replied, his voice thick with emotion.

The family gathered outside the hospital, near the ambulance, as it prepared to take Jesse and Mel back to Ohio. The air was thick with a mixture of relief and lingering tension, everyone acutely aware that the past few days had been an emotional rollercoaster.

"Safe travels," Marco called out, giving a small wave as the ambulance's engine roared to life. Beth and Cole exchanged somber looks, their eyes reflecting the shared weight of the ordeal they'd just experienced.

"Jesse's a tough old bird," Chloe murmured, trying to inject some lightness into the atmosphere. "He'll pull through this, you'll see."

As the ambulance pulled away, disappearing around a bend in the road, Faye couldn't help but release a shaky breath she hadn't realized she'd been holding. She turned to her friend, seeking the comfort of Chloe's steady presence.

"Chloe... I don't know what I would have done without you these past days," Faye admitted, her voice quivering with raw emotion. "Your strength and support... it means the world to me."

"Darlin', we're family," Chloe replied, wrapping her arms around Faye in a warm embrace. "That's what families do—we stick together through thick and thin."

Faye leaned into the hug, grateful for the solid grounding Chloe offered. As they stood there, the sun dipped below the horizon, casting long shadows across the hospital grounds. A moment of peace settled over them, providing a brief respite from the turmoil of recent events.

"Jesse has a long road ahead," Faye said quietly, pulling away from Chloe and wiping away a stray tear. "But he's strong, and so are we. We'll get through this together."

"Absolutely," Chloe agreed, squeezing Faye's hand reassuringly. "And remember, you've got all of us behind you every step of the way."

Faye nodded, drawing strength from Chloe's words. Though the future remained uncertain, she knew that with her family by her side–and friends like Chloe–they would find a way to navigate the challenges that lay ahead.

"Thank you, Chloe," Faye whispered, her voice full of gratitude. "For everything."

"Anytime, darlin'," Chloe replied, her eyes shining with affection. "Anytime at all."

CHAPTER 18

The car carrying the weary travelers rolled to a stop, the engine sputtering before falling silent. The air was crisp and cool–a welcome change from the stifling humidity they had left behind in Tennessee.

"Feels good to be back," Dana said as she stepped out of the driver's seat, stretching her thin frame. Her eyes were heavy with exhaustion, but there was an unmistakable sense of relief in them as well.

"Tell me about it," Hannah replied, her own tired features lighting up with a grateful smile. She unbuckled Jef from his car-seat, then reached into the trunk of the car and unloaded their bags, the weight of the recent events still showing in her movements. "I didn't realize how much I missed Morelville until now."

"Neither did I." Dana joined Hannah, her extra pair of hands making quick work of the luggage. As they carried their belongings toward the front door, the events of the past week replayed in Dana's mind. The murders, the accusations against Cole, the race against time to find the actual killer–it had all been almost too much to bear. And yet, here they were, home safe and sound.

"Think everything will go back to normal now?" Hannah asked, breaking the silence that had fallen between them.

"God, I hope so." Dana heaved a sigh, trying not to let her weariness show too much. "We've all been through enough, don't you think?"

Hannah nodded, her grip on the suitcase handle tightening momentarily. "Yeah, we have.

Cole and Beth stepped out of the car at their house, next door to Dana and Mel's house, their young faces weighed down by fatigue and a lingering tension that seemed to have settled into their bones. As they reached for the bags in the trunk, their gazes met briefly, acknowledging the shared burden of recent events.

"Here, let me grab that one," Cole said, gesturing to a particularly heavy suitcase. Beth nodded silently, allowing her older brother to take charge.

Together, they carried their family's belongings up the front steps and into the house, their footsteps echoing softly through the quiet hallway. The familiar scent of home wafted around them, and Cole couldn't help but feel a small sense of relief seeping through the cracks of his exhaustion - at least they were safe now.

"Where should we put these?" Beth asked, her voice barely above a whisper.

"Let's just get them out of the way for now," Cole suggested, nodding towards the living room. "We can sort them out later."

As they carefully set the suitcases down, their mother, Kris, and stepfather Lance appeared in the doorway, their faces visibly relieved as they took in their surroundings.

"Finally, home to our own bed," Lance murmured with a weary smile, wrapping an arm around his wife's shoulders.

"Can't wait," Kris agreed, leaning into her husband's embrace. "I don't think I've ever been this tired in my life."

"Go on, you two," Cole urged, trying to inject some lightness into his voice. "We'll take care of things down here."

"Thank you, but it's still a little early, and I want to get out to the farm and check on your grandpa," Kris told her eldest.

"Oh. We should go too, Beth said. We promised to help with the chores."

Kris waved her daughter off. "We're home a day early and the guys who were taking care of everything while we were gone are out there. It can wait until morning."

When his mother left, Cole collapsed onto the couch, finally allowing himself a moment to simply exist without the weight of suspicion and fear pressing down on him. Beth sank down beside him, her gaze fixed on the floor as she chewed her lip, lost in thought.

"Hey," Cole nudged his sister gently, "we made it through this. We're home now, and things will get better."

"I know," Beth whispered, her eyes filling with tears as she looked up at her brother. "But it's just... so much happened, Cole. I can't help but wonder what's next for us."

"Whatever it is," Cole promised, his voice firm with conviction, "we'll face it together. Just like we always have."

"Promise?" Beth asked, her voice small and vulnerable.

"Promise."

Faye watched as Kris pulled away after stopping by to see her father and to help Mel unload Jesse's car.

Even though she was exhausted, she could already feel the familiar pull of routine calling to her like a siren's song. With a determined nod, she rolled up her sleeves and began to unpack all their luggage and to move through the house, putting things away, and tidying up as well, as she went.

"Mom, you don't need to do that right now," Mel said, concern etching her face as she watched Faye flit from one task to the next.

"Melissa, I've got this," Faye replied, her movements crisp and efficient as she plucked a stray magazine from the coffee table. "Your father is asleep, and you've got his next round of medication all set up. There's nothing for me to do there right now. You know how I am; I need to keep busy."

"Alright, just don't overdo it," Mel conceded, knowing there was no stopping her mother once she set her mind to something.

Faye's hands flew as she worked, the rhythmic motion of wiping down countertops and rearranging knick-knacks soothing her frazzled nerves. In the background, she could hear a car coming up the drive and Mel's footsteps receding towards the front door.

Stepping onto the porch, Mel filled her lungs with the earthy scent of Ohio air, letting the breeze tousle her short-cropped hair while she watched Dana's car come up the drive. A sense of peace washed over her, the weight of recent events momentarily lifting from her shoulders. As she leaned against the railing, she couldn't help but think of how lucky they were after all they'd been through that they had all made it back home safely.

"Feels good to be home, huh?" Dana asked, when she joined her wife on the porch.

"More than you can imagine," Mel murmured, reaching out to take Dana's hand. The warmth of her wife's palm anchored her, reminding her that whatever challenges life threw their way, they would face them together.

"Dad's sleeping," Mel told her. "Everyone all settled in at home?"

"Hannah was starting laundry when I left and Jef was asking for Boo and digging through all his toys. Hannah and I are exhausted, but he slept the last two hours of the trip, so he's primed for action."

Mel grinned. "There's not much you can do here, so you might as well go on home and rest. Mom's fighting her tiredness by cleaning. I'll stay tonight and Kris will stay tomorrow. We'll figure it out after that, but I think we'll be in the clear to leave him with just mom at night after tomorrow. Chloe will help too."

"As will I," Dana said. "And I'm not leaving just yet. With everything that's happened the last several days, we haven't had a chance to just be together at all."

"Can't argue with that."

Inside the house, Faye continued her cleaning spree, allowing the familiar routine to ground her. She paused for a moment, listening to the hum of the low conversation between Mel and Dana on the porch punctuated by Jesse's snoring in their bedroom off the living room.

"Everyone's home and everyone's safe," she whispered to herself, feeling a sense of calm settle over her like a warm blanket. "We're all back where we belong."

With renewed purpose, Faye plunged back into her tasks, eager to reclaim the normalcy that had been so elusive in recent weeks.

Dusk was settling over the village when Cole wrenched his old bicycle out of the shed and rode it out to the farm.

When he got there, he avoided the farmhouse where he could see Dana's car parked alongside his grandfather's Sunday car, opting instead for the barn. As he pushed open the heavy wooden doors, the scent of hay and horses immediately filled his nostrils, bringing with it a wave of comfort and familiarity. He didn't know why, but being around these animals always had a calming effect on him.

"Hey there, Thunder," he murmured, reaching out to stroke the velvety nose of his favorite horse. The animal nickered softly in response, sensing his rider's emotional turmoil.

"Man, what a mess, huh?" Cole sighed, resting his forehead against Thunder's broad neck. "I never thought I'd be so glad to be back here in Morelville."

The horse snorted, as if offering his understanding and support. Cole couldn't help but smile at the simple act of connection.

"Guess I just needed some time away from everything," he continued, his voice barely audible even to himself. "Just you and me for a little while, okay? I need you right now, buddy."

As Cole confided in his equine friend out at the farm, finding solace in the connection they shared, back at home Beth sat cross-legged on her bed, her eyes closed as she tried to process the tumultuous emotions swirling within her. From anger to fear, relief to weariness, each feeling rose and fell like waves crashing against the shore of her consciousness.

"Things will get better," she whispered to herself, her grip tightening around a small, worn teddy bear. "We're home now. We're safe."

The warm glow of the kitchen lights in the farmhouse illuminated Mel and Dana as they sat down at the worn wooden table, their hands clasped tightly together. The scent of fresh coffee brewing filled the air, an aroma that was both comforting and familiar.

The calm silence between them was punctuated only by the ticking of the old kitchen clock mounted on the wall. As the seconds passed, Mel could feel the weight of everything they'd been through–the fear, the uncertainty, the danger–lift from her shoulders. She squeezed Dana's hand gently, the simple gesture speaking volumes about their bond.

"Thank you," she whispered, her voice barely audible. "For being there, for being strong... for being my rock."

"Always, my love," Dana replied, her eyes shining with unshed tears. "We've faced so much together, haven't we? And we've always come out stronger."

Mel nodded, taking a deep breath as she leaned back in her chair, feeling the warmth of their connection settle around her like a protective cloak.

Jesse, his legs propped up on a nearby footrest, watched the scene unfolding in the kitchen from his favorite armchair in the living room. He couldn't help but feel a swell of pride and gratitude as he observed the love and strength that bound his family together.

"Y'all made it through some tough times," he murmured, more to himself than anyone else. "And here you are, we all are, back home safe and sound. Lord knows I'm grateful for that."

His gaze drifted over to the framed photographs on the mantelpiece, each one capturing a cherished memory from happier times. Jesse knew that, despite everything they had endured, those moments were the ones that truly defined his family.

"Sometimes, I forget how strong we Cranes are," he mused, a weak but genuine smile playing on his lips. "But then I see you all together, supporting each other, and I remember."

With her father's words, Mel felt a sense of clarity washing over her. It was time to make a change, one that had been long overdue. She pulled out her phone, dialed Todd Bell's number, and took a deep breath as it rang.

"Hey, Todd," she said, her voice firm. "I've made a decision. I'm stepping down as Sheriff. SGT Gates should take my place."

"Are you sure about this, Mel?" Todd asked, concern lacing his words.

"Positive," Mel replied, her gaze flicking to Dana, who offered her a supportive nod. "I'll give you up to six months to get him trained, but it's time for me to focus on what really matters–my family."

"Alright," Todd sighed. "I'll start the process with the mayor of getting him appointed as interim sheriff, and we'll get the county clerk to work on setting up a special election. Take care of yourself, Mel."

"Thanks, Todd. I appreciate it." With that, Mel ended the call and slipped the phone back into her pocket. A weight seemed to lift from her shoulders, leaving her feeling lighter than she had in years.

Despite their tiredness at the lack of sleep and long road trip, the farmhouse living room filled with people and the sounds of laughter and conversation, as the Crane and Rossi families gathered together.

Faye handed out mugs of steaming coffee to everyone but Jesse and the kids, her movements fluid and practiced, while Jesse shared stories from his younger days, his voice still weak but filled with warmth and humor.

"Remember that time we tried to ride that old bull, Mel?" Jesse chuckled, his eyes twinkling with mischief. "Darn near broke our necks, didn't we?"

"Speak for yourself, Dad," Mel retorted, grinning at the memory. "I stayed on for a whole eight seconds!"

"Eight seconds? More like two!" Cole chimed in, his laughter infectious. The room erupted with laughter, the tension from their recent ordeal dissipating with each shared recollection.

As the evening progressed, Mel sank into the familiar rhythms of family life, the love and camaraderie that had always been her anchor. She glanced around the room, taking in the faces of those she held dear–Dana's warm smile, Chloe's animated gestures, Cole and Beth's quiet but genuine laughter.

For the first time in what felt like an eternity, Mel allowed herself to believe that they could all find their way back to normalcy, to the peace and happiness that Morelville had once offered them.

CHAPTER 19

Muskingum County Sheriff's Department

Mel strode into her office on Monday morning with a furrowed brow and a steaming cup of black coffee in hand. The room was small and mostly unadorned, but functional with only a framed map of the county hung on one wall as decoration. She took her usual seat behind the cluttered wooden desk, setting down her mug and taking off the reading glasses she hated to wear to rub at the bridge of her nose.

"Alright, Shane, Janet, have a seat," she commanded, her deep voice tinged with the exhaustion that came from long hours spent on a perplexing case. Shane and Janet obliged, pulling up chairs across from their formidable leader. Their expressions mirrored hers - determined, yet weary.

"Let's go over what we've got so far on this body-in-the-trunk case," Mel began, sinking back into her chair as she steepled her fingers in thought. "We need to make sure we're not missing anything."

"Sounds good, boss," Shane replied, flipping open his notepad. He was a lanky man in his early thirties, with short-cropped hair and a curious gaze that seemed to take in every detail of the world around him.

"First off," Janet chimed in, pushing a strand of long hair back behind her ear as she glanced at her own notes, "We found fingerprints on the trunk of the car that don't match your brother-in-law or the guy who owned the lot it was sitting on. We've sent them off to the Columbus Crime Lab for analysis, but no matches in the system so far."

"Keep an eye on that," Mel instructed, her mind already racing with the implications of this evidence. "If we can't find a match, we'll need to broaden our search parameters."

"Got it," Shane nodded, making a note on his pad.

"Next, we have the DNA samples," Janet continued, shuffling through the papers on the desk before her. "They were collected from under the fingernails of Greg Foster and sent to the crime lab as well. They're pretty backed up, so we're still waiting on the lab results for those, but we should have them within the next day or two."

"Good," Mel acknowledged, feeling a spark of hope that something in those samples might lead them to answers. "And what about his family? What do we know?"

"Ah, yes," Shane said, adjusting his glasses as he glanced at his notes. "We talked to his sister, Nadine Hemming. Not a lot of help. It's just the two of them in the world. Their mother was a single mother who was an only child. Her parents are deceased, as is she. Cancer last year. Foster was divorced, no kids. Nadine is also divorced, one child, a son, age 11 that Foster doted on."

He went on. "Nadine and Foster talked occasionally, texted often, and had a habit of getting together for dinner the last Sunday of every month, rotating who cooked or bought. This month she and her son went to Foster's place. They had confirmed with each other on

Saturday, but he never answered the door on Sunday. She had a key and went inside. No one was home, nothing was amiss. She messaged him a few times. No response. She was pretty broken up when she heard he was murdered and seemed as mystified as we are that anyone would want him dead."

"Any love interest for Greg Foster?" Mel asked.

Janet shook her head. "A few months prior, he brought a woman he was dating to Sunday dinner with his sister, but they broke up a week later. Nadine said he had mentioned no one else since. She said his divorce was amicable. The ex-wife lives in Chicago now and hasn't factored into his life in a few years."

"Did you get a look at his...house...apartment?"

"House in Reynoldsburg," Shane answered. "Yes. Not your typical bachelor pad. Sister says he was a neat freak, and it shows."

Mel leaned back in her chair. "So, no sign the murder happened there?"

"No," Janet said. "The place was spotless, but we did dust for prints. Nothing lifted there that didn't match him, and nothing particularly heavy he could have been hit with for the death blow."

"Employer?"

Shane answered, "Self employed as a technical writer. Worked out of his house doing a lot of work for medical device manufacturers. According to Nadine, he had a degree in English Lit with a minor in journalism from Otterbein."

"Drug habit?"

"Tox was negative," Janet replied. "Nadine said he didn't smoke or drink either."

Mel let out a sigh. "So, we've got a basically clean-cut guy who lives a quiet life, with no known enemies, who dies in an unknown place by blunt force trauma, and then is left in the trunk of a classic car forty-some miles from his home."

Shane and Janet both nodded.

"And no video where the car was, no witnesses, and no signs of a struggle other than what was under his nails." She was reciting what they knew, so Shane and Janet just nodded.

Mel stood and turned toward her window. "The more we learn, the less we know. Seems our perp was being extra cautious," Mel mused, as she considered their frustrating lack of leads. Her thoughts drifted momentarily to her wife, Dana, and their cabin in the Smoky Mountains. She longed for the simplicity and serenity they found there, away from the grim reality of cases like this.

"Alright," Mel said, shaking off her momentary reverie and refocusing on the task at hand. "Let's get back to work. We won't let this case go cold. Find that ex-girlfriend. Find out how they met. Find his friends. Somebody has to know something that will give us a lead."

"Agreed," Shane and Janet said in unison, determination etched on their faces as they prepared to delve deeper into the mystery of the body in the trunk that was Greg Foster.

Mel leaned back in her chair, the worn leather creaking beneath her weight. She stared at the photos of a very dead Greg Foster and his final resting place spread across her desk, each gruesome detail serving as a reminder of the urgency of their investigation. Her gaze lingered on the image of the victim's lifeless hand dangling from the trunk, the DNA beneath his nails the only lead they still had. She wondered if Todd had any pull with that section of the crime lab.

Mel watched the pair leave before reaching for her phone. As she dialed the coroner's office, her thoughts drifted to the victim, wondering what secrets and stories were hidden behind their now-silent lips.

"Hey, it's Mel Crane," she said when the line connected. "I'm calling about the Foster case. Do we have any new information on the cause of death or distinguishing features?"

As she waited, her fingers tapped rhythmically on the cool surface of her desk. Finally, the voice on the other end spoke, providing her with the details she sought.

"Blunt force trauma hard enough to cause instant death. The object was smooth. There was no laceration to the head," the coroner confirmed. "And there's a small tattoo on the victim's left ankle–a crescent moon intertwined with some sort of vine."

"Interesting," Mel murmured, jotting down the information. The tattoo could be significant, a lead to follow if they discovered anything unusual about Greg Foster in life. "Email me a picture of the tattoo please, and thanks for the update."

***

Detective Mason pulled up once again to the modest two-story house belonging to Nadine Hemming, Greg Foster's sister. It had been two days since her initial interview with Nadine, but Mel, Shane, and Janet all still had unanswered questions about Greg's life and relationships.

She stepped out of her cruiser into the chill autumn air. Making her way up the front walkway, she hoped Nadine would have additional details to aid the investigation.

Janet rang the bell and offered a sympathetic smile when Nadine appeared, face weary and eyes swollen from crying.

"Mrs. Hemming, I'm sorry to bother you again so soon," Janet said gently. "But I was hoping we could talk a bit more about your brother. There are still some gaps we're trying to fill in."

"Of course, Detective, please come in," Nadine replied, dabbing at her eyes with a tissue as she led Janet inside. "I'm sorry. The coroner released his body this morning. I've just been tending to burial arrangements."

"I'm so sorry. I promise not to keep you too long."

Once seated in the living room, Janet pulled out her notebook. "I recall you said your brother Greg had brought a woman named Lynn to dinner a few months back. Do you happen to remember her last name or how they met?"

"Let me think..." Nadine grabbed her phone and began scrolling back through old messages and social media posts. After a few moments, she said "Ah, here it is! Her name was Lynn Tricoli."

Nadine turned the phone to show Janet the woman's Facebook profile. "As for how they met, I'm not really sure. Greg didn't share many details and I didn't pry. I believe she was an acquaintance of an old college friend."

Janet nodded, making note of the name and profile. "What was your impression of her?"

"Well, Lynn seemed nice enough when she and Greg came over, but I could tell the relationship wasn't very serious," Nadine recalled. "She was a bit reserved, not very affectionate with Greg. I wasn't surprised when they stopped seeing each other after just a couple of months. It didn't appear to be a strong connection."

Looking back at the screen, Nadine shook her head. "No, I highly doubt Lynn had anything to do with...what happened to Greg. They parted ways amicably as far as I know."

"That's good to hear," Janet replied. "We just need to explore every possibility." She thanked Nadine again for the information before taking her leave, mind spinning with the new lead.

Can I ask, Can you recall any of Greg's current friends or regular contacts?"

Nadine shook her head sadly. "Greg didn't have many close friends that I knew of. A few old college buddies he texted occasionally, but no one local he saw regularly."

"What about coworkers from his last job, before he went out on his own?" Janet pressed. "Did he hang out with anyone from there?"

"Well, not really," Nadine admitted. "There was some kind of harassment issue between two other employees. Greg tried to stay out of it, but they involved him even after he left the company."

Janet jotted this down. "Do you happen to recall the names of those former coworkers?"

"Let me think..." Nadine pondered for a moment. "Jessica something, I believe. And there was a man too, George or Gerald?"

"That's very helpful," Janet assured her. "Even just first names may aid our investigation." She spent the next twenty minutes gently prodding Nadine for any other details about her brother's life and social circles, hoping to shake loose new information.

Finally, sensing Nadine's exhaustion, Janet closed her notebook and stood. "Thank you again, Mrs. Hemming. I know these discussions dredge up painful memories, but you've helped point us in key directions."

"I just want Greg's killer found," Nadine said tearfully as she started to show Janet out.

As Janet prepared to leave, a thought occurred to her. "Mrs. Hemming, I have one more question. Our coroner noticed your brother had a small tattoo of a crescent moon on his ankle and maybe some ivy or something across it. Do you happen to know the significance of it?"

Nadine pondered for a moment before her eyes lit up. "Oh, that silly old thing! I had forgotten about it completely." She let out a sad chuckle. "Greg got that tattoo during college after a night out with friends. It was an impulsive decision. His one concession to the 'wild life,' he once cracked about it."

"Did it symbolize anything specific?" Janet pressed gently. "Even a minor detail could be helpful."

"Well..." Nadine thought hard. "I believe Greg chose the moon because he was an avid bird watcher. He loved being out early to spot birds at dawn or dusk, so the moon reminded him of those peaceful times. What you're looking at as ivy is probably some small birds. As I recall, it's a very small tattoo."

Janet quickly jotted this down. "That's very insightful, thank you. Greg's hobby wasn't known to us yet."

"Of course," Nadine replied. "Greg loved photographing birds and could identify them by sound. He was involved with the Audubon Society and often volunteered at wildlife preserves. I hope that detail aids your investigation."

"It certainly provides valuable context," Janet assured her. She made a mental note to explore the victim's involvement with birding communities, which could yield potential leads. With this new tattoo insight, she had one more pivotal piece of the puzzle.

"We will find them," Janet promised before making her way to her cruiser, new leads swirling in her mind. She now had a specific ex-girlfriend to track down, as well as former coworkers who may have harbored grudges against the victim. Turning the keys in the ignition, Janet set off to follow these promising new threads in the hopes of unraveling this tragic mystery.

***

The smell of fresh bread and coffee enveloped Janet as she stepped into the Hilliard bakery. Scanning the counter area, she spotted her target – the owner Lynn Tricoli - seated alone at a table by the window drinking a cup of coffee.

Janet approached, badge in hand. "Ms. Tricoli? I'm Detective Janet Mason, Muskingum County Sheriff's Department. Do you have a moment to speak about Greg Foster?"

Lynn's eyes widened in surprise. "Greg? Of course, have a seat." She gestured to the empty chair across from her. "Is everything okay?"

"Actually, I'm afraid not," Janet said gently as she sat down. "Greg was found deceased under suspicious circumstances. We're speaking with those close to him to aid our investigation."

"Oh my goodness, that's horrible!" Lynn gasped, hand flying to her mouth. After a moment to compose herself, she shook her head. "Greg was a really nice guy, but we were never serious. Just a few casual dates."

Janet nodded, retrieving her notebook. "How did you and Greg meet?"

"Through a mutual friend, Peter Hanson," Lynn explained. "Peter's a college buddy of Greg's that I dated briefly too. It didn't work out, and Peter actually introduced me to Greg. Thought we might hit it off."

"Was there any jealousy there, with you moving on to Greg?" Janet questioned.

Lynn laughed lightly. "No, Peter was very gracious about it. He knew we ultimately weren't right for each other."

"Why's that?" Janet inquired.

Lynn smiled sadly. "Well, Peter is a great guy, but he has special needs that require a big commitment. A bit too much for me at this stage of life. But he wanted me to be happy, so he connected me with Greg who shared some of my interests."

Janet jotted notes hastily, intrigued by this dynamic. "Such as?"

"We're both big readers, love being outdoors. Peter thought we'd click but..." Lynn trailed off.

"But?" Janet pressed.

"Don't get me wrong, Greg was very sweet," Lynn said. "But our lifestyles were too different. His favorite hobby was birdwatching. Nice for him, but not my cup of tea. We parted on good terms."

"I see," Janet nodded. "And you don't know of any conflict Greg had with Peter or anyone else?"

"None at all," Lynn confirmed.

"Well, thank you for your time, Ms. Tricoli," Janet said, standing to leave. "You've given me a good starting point. Would you happen to have contact information for Peter Hanson?"

"Of course!" Lynn grabbed a napkin, checked her phone, and jotted down Peter's number. "I hope you find whoever did this to Greg."

"We will," Janet assured her before stepping back out into the cold autumn air, new lead in hand.

***

The squeaking of Peter Hanson's wheelchair punctuated the silence as he led Janet through the front door of his modest ranch-style home.

"Make yourself comfortable, detective," Peter offered, gesturing towards the plush sofa. "Can I get you some coffee?"

"No thank you, Mr. Hanson," Janet replied, taking a seat and retrieving her notebook. Her eyes scanned the lived-in space, toys and books scattered about indicating children frequented the home.

Peter wheeled himself to face Janet, curiosity mingled with unease on his bespectacled face. "How can I help?"

"I'm investigating the death of Greg Foster," Janet began gently. "I understand you two were friends in college?"

Peter's face fell. "Greg is...dead? My god, that's horrible. Such a good man." He removed his glasses, wiping away tears.

Janet gave him a moment before continuing. "I'm very sorry for your loss. Anything you can share about Greg's life or relationships would aid our investigation."

Composing himself, Peter nodded. "Of course, of course. Greg was one of my only true friends back then. Most people just saw the wheelchair and avoided me. But not Greg."

"How did you meet?" Janet asked.

"Freshman dorms," Peter recalled fondly. "We were neighbors and hit it off right away over our shared love of books and the outdoors."

Janet smiled encouragingly, hoping to keep Peter talking.

"Greg didn't care that I was different," Peter went on. "He looked past the chair and treated me like anyone else. I'll always cherish that."

"It sounds like he was a good man," Janet affirmed. "Did you stay in touch after college?"

"Here and there," Peter said. "Life pulls people in different directions, but we'd text occasionally about books or to reminisce. I can't imagine anyone wanting to hurt him though."

Janet weighed how to delicately bring up Lynn. "I understand you also knew Lynn Tricoli, and introduced her to Greg?"

Peter's expression warmed. "Ah, Lynn. A lovely woman, but not destined for me. She deserved someone who could...be there fully, so I connected her with Greg. They seemed fond of each other for a time."

"But it didn't last?" Janet pressed.

"Sadly no," Peter sighed. "I think their lifestyles were too disparate, but they parted amicably."

Janet jotted notes hastily, hoping to uncover anything that could explain the bizarre murder of Greg Foster. As the conversation deepened, she found herself believing more and more that Peter truly had no clue why anyone would harm his good-natured friend. But she had to be sure; people could deceive, even unwittingly.

"Are there any other friends of Greg's you're aware of, we could talk to?"

Peter started to shake his head but stopped himself. "David Bennett, maybe? Greg mentioned him once several months back. They might have been keeping in touch."

"Any idea how to contact him?"

"Sorry. We were never close. I didn't keep in touch with him after college."

***

When Janet stepped back into the cramped space she shared with her fellow detective Shane Harding, he glanced up from a file he was reviewing. "Any luck tracking down leads on Foster?"

"A few promising threads," Janet replied, sinking into her swivel chair with a sigh. "But we need to find someone who was close to him in his current life. The ex and old college buddy didn't yield much."

She quickly relayed the details of her conversations with Nadine, Lynn and Peter, watching Shane jot down notes.

"There was one name that came up - David Bennett," Janet continued. "Apparently a friend of Greg's that Peter mentioned. But no contact info, and it's a pretty common name."

Shane nodded along thoughtfully as he flipped through a BMV database. There are two in the Reynoldsburg area. Could be one of them."

Janet's eyes lit up. "That's a great start! Let's cross-reference and see if we get any social media connections or other ties to Foster."

The two detectives spent the next hour combing through search results and social media profiles of the three David Bennetts, searching for any link to their victim. After digging through hundreds of online photos and posts, a connection finally emerged.

"Bingo! Look here," Shane said, angling his computer screen towards Janet. "David Bennett the third co-managed a birdwatching Facebook group with Greg Foster over the past two years. They led hikes and workshops together."

"That's got to be our guy!" Janet exclaimed, feeling a rush of excitement. "Greg's sister said he was into birding, and that's what his tattoo represented."

"Exactly," Shane agreed, already scribbling down the contact information listed on the group's page. "I'll run this number and get an address. You want to pay Mr. Bennett a visit tomorrow?"

"First thing," Janet confirmed, feeling reenergized by this promising new lead. Any friend close enough to share Greg's niche birdwatching hobby had to have insight into his life and habits.

As she gathered her things to head home for the night, Janet's mind raced with questions for this David Bennett: How long had he known Greg Foster? Did they socialize outside of the birding group? Had

Greg confided in him about any conflicts or fears? She needed to uncover if this man held any clues that could blow open their languishing
murder investigation.

"See you bright and early," Shane called after her as she headed out
the door into the darkened parking lot, the glow of the streetlights
ushering her to her car. Janet waved an acknowledging hand, hope
rising within her. She couldn't wait to chase down this promising
thread.

***

The Next Morning

"It's a bust," Janet told Shane. The David Bennett Peter said Greg
was talking to him about was around Greg's age, 34. The David Bennett we dug up yesterday is 79.

"It can't be a coincidence," Shane replied. "What are the odds?"

"It really is a common name."

"What is?" Mel asked as she entered their office with a stack of
papers.

"David Bennett. We thought we had a potential lead for the foster
case but it appears we might be wrong."

"I know a David Bennett," Mel said. "Lives in Dresden. He married
an ex-Amish lady and they have a passel of kids."

Janet wrinkled her nose. "He's probably not our guy either unless
he's around 34 and went to Otterbein."

"Nope. He'd be in his late forties."

"Not our guy," Shane said. He pointed at the stack of papers Mel
held. "What's all that?"

She dropped them on his desk as she responded, "Paper phone records for Foster. They just came in." She reached into the pocket of her uniform shirt and pulled out a thumb drive. "We have them digital too."

Shane and Janet sat hunched over the victim's phone records. While Shane rifled through the paper stack, Janet opted for digital, the blue glow of her computer screen casting an eerie shadow across her face. The hum of the air circulating system filled the room as they scanned through the data, searching for any telltale patterns or connections.

"Look at this," Janet said, pointing to a series of calls made to the same number in the days leading up to the murder. She waited while Shane looked through her screen. "Whoever this is, they spoke to our victim for nearly two hours, total."

"Could be a lover, a friend, or even an accomplice," Shane mused, scribbling down the number on his notepad. "Let's see if we can find anything on social media."

While her detectives delved deeper into the digital world, Mel returned to her office. She paced back and forth, her mind racing with possibilities. She knew that every minute mattered, and she refused to let the case grow cold. Picking up the phone, she dialed the forensic lab's number and waited to be put through to the department head for trace evidence.

"Dr. Higgins? This is Sheriff Crane," she said, her voice firm but fair when he came on the line. "I really need you to prioritize the DNA evidence from the body-in-the-trunk case. The victim has been ID'd as Greg Foster. We don't have a lead on the perp, but there are those scrapings from his nails that might give us something. We're hoping you can give us something that helps to connect the dots."

"Of course, Sheriff," Dr. Higgins replied, sensing the urgency in Mel's tone. "We'll have the results to you as soon as possible."

"Thank you, Doctor." Mel hung up the phone, her heart pounding. Time was of the essence.

Back downstairs, in their cramped office, Shane and Janet continued their investigation, poring over the victim's phone records, and his Facebook and Instagram accounts. They discovered photos of birds and trees, and several of Nadine and a boy-presumably Nadine's son-in seemingly happy moments, but nothing that immediately pointed to a motive for murder.

"Maybe we're looking at this the wrong way," Janet suggested, rubbing her eyes. "What if the key isn't in the people our victim knew, but in the people he didn't know?"

"Strangers?" Shane raised an eyebrow. "That's a bit of a long shot, but I suppose we have to consider all possibilities."

"Exactly," Janet agreed. "Let's go back through the phone records and cross-reference them with the social media accounts. Maybe we'll find something we missed."

***

Mel's mouth twisted into a grim line as she leaned back against her desk, arms crossed, waiting for Shane and Janet to present their list of potential suspects.

"Alright," Shane began, his eyes glued to a notepad filled with scribbles. "We cross-referenced the name Peter gave Janet, David Bennett, with the victim's phone records and his social media accounts, and with known associates and came up with him and six other names that stood out."

"Six? That's it?" Mel frowned, tapping her fingers impatiently on the desk. Her gut told her the answer was close, but it felt like they were grasping at straws. "Who do we have?"

"First off, we did find the right David Bennett. He's been living out of state the past four months, and we've ruled him out. There are three other former college classmates, two former coworkers, and a neighbor who had a few run-ins with the victim," Janet explained, producing photos and printouts from a manila folder. "We dug into their socials, too, where any existed. All had some friction with the victim, but nothing that screams 'murderer' just yet."

"Let's brainstorm," Mel said, straightening herself and moving around her desk to take her seat. "We need to prioritize these leads and figure out where to focus our efforts."

"Agreed," Shane nodded, spreading the evidence across the desk. "We'll start with the college classmates. First up, this guy, Derek Jacobs. He's got a history of anger issues, but no criminal record. By the looks of things, their connection continues across social media only. He lives in Eastern Pennsylvania."

"Next is Sarah Matthews," Janet continued. "She's been posting some cryptic messages online lately, but nothing directly related to the victim. Still, worth keeping an eye on."

"Lastly, there's Alex Thompson," Shane added. "They dated for an even shorter time than he dated the last woman —

"Lynn," Janet supplied.

"Thanks. They split up over a year ago, but Foster kept in touch with a couple of Thomspon's family members. Could be something there."

"Or," Mel put in, "he knew her family first and they introduced them."

"True. That fits what we know about how he meets women and his dating habits," Shane said.

"What about the former coworkers?" Mel asked. She knew they couldn't afford to overlook any detail.

"Jessica Smith and Gary Newman," Janet replied. "They all worked together at a marketing company until Foster left and started freelancing. Jessica reported Gary for harassment and named Foster as a witness, but it was never officially resolved. Newman left the company. Smith still works there."

"Dig into that," Mel instructed. "Now, the neighbor?"

"Ah, yes," Shane said, shifting through his notes. "Maddie Turner. She's had a few noise complaints against our victim, but no direct confrontations."

"Noise?" Mel asked.

"Loud music."

"Seems out of character for him." Mel sighed and rubbed her temples as she weighed their options. "It's a start, but we need to dig deeper. Look for any hidden motives or connections between these people, especially those former co-workers. We can't let this case go cold."

"Understood, Sheriff," Shane replied. Janet nodded her understanding.

As the three of them continued to piece together the puzzle, Mel couldn't shake the feeling that something vital was missing – something crucial. A key detail that could break the case wide open. But until they found it, they would keep pushing forward.

"Alright, let's go over this one more time," she said, pulling herself upright. "We need to be sure we've covered every angle."

"Agreed," Shane replied, his determination evident in his voice. Janet nodded again but kept her eyes fixed on their list of potential suspects.

How much help were those phone records tracking any of these people down?" Mel asked,

"He spent the better part of two hours on the phone with someone we've been able to determine is a technical writing client in the days prior to his death. There's nothing out of the ordinary beyond that, but I'm still digging," Janet responded.

"Okay," Mel sighed, her hands coming together in a steeple beneath her chin. "That seems like a no longer viable route often times. People don't call each other anymore."

"But," Shane said, "they do text. We don't have those records, yet."

Mel grimaced. "Well, in the meantime, I want you two to look into those former coworkers and the neighbor. See if there's anything that ties them further to our victim."

"Will do, Sheriff," Janet said, already gathering her things to leave.

"Remember," Mel called after them as they headed towards the door, "we're dealing with someone who thought they could get away with murder. They won't make it easy for us. Stay focused and stay safe."

"Understood," Shane and Janet chorused, determination etched on their faces.

Mel watched as they left the office, and then turned back to the crime board she'd hung over the map on her wall, her eyes scanning every detail. Her mind raced with possibilities and theories, but none seemed to fit the puzzle quite right.

"Damn it," she muttered under her breath, frustration building in her chest. "What are we missing?"

She knew they were close - so close to finding the answers they needed to solve this case. But as the night wore on, and the room grew darker, Mel was left with an uneasy feeling that threatened to consume her.

"Melissa Crane," she whispered to herself, her eyes narrowing with resolve. "You've faced tougher cases than this. Get it together."

CHAPTER 20

S heriff Mel Crane leaned back in her office chair, sighing deeply. The murder of Greg Foster had hit yet another dead end. Without a murder weapon or suspects with clear motive, she was at a loss.

A sharp rap at her open door broke the silence. Detectives Janet Mason and Shane Harding entered, files in hand.

"Please tell me you've got something new," Mel implored. "We're spinning our wheels on this one."

"A promising lead, finally," Janet offered. She opened the file, sliding a photo across Mel's desk. "Meet Gary Newman, Foster's former coworker."

Mel straightened. "Go on."

"There was an office harassment scandal at their old workplace between two other employees," Shane explained. "Foster witnessed it and was named by the complainant, though he had already left the company."

"HR investigated but couldn't corroborate the allegations," Janet added. "However, this Newman still lost his job. His other former coworkers say he's held a major grudge against Foster ever since."

Mel's eyes narrowed. "Where is Newman now?"

"Here's the kicker - public records show he relocated to Zanesville a few months back." Shane raised a brow meaningfully.

"Right before Foster was murdered," Mel realized. "What's his address? We need to question this guy ASAP."

Thirty minutes later, Mel stood on Newman's doorstep flanked by her detectives. A burly, unshaven man answered.

"Gary Newman?" Mel flashed her badge. "I'm Sheriff Crane. We need to talk about Greg Foster."

Panic flashed across Newman's face before he scowled. "Haven't seen Foster in ages. Don't know nothing about him."

He moved to slam the door, but Mel wedged her foot in. "Not so fast. You're going to tell us exactly where you were the night of March 14th."

"Don't remember, that was weeks ago." Newman muttered. "Home, probably."

Mel withdrew a photo - his social media post from that night about visiting a wildlife area. Newman paled.

"That true?" Mel pressed. "You were at the wildlife center the night Greg Foster was killed?"

"Alright, fine! I was there," Newman conceded. "But I didn't hurt anyone. I went home after."

Mel's eyes bored into him. "I think you're lying. In fact, I believe you followed Foster from there and killed him in a rage."

"You're crazy!" Newman shouted, but panic flashed in his eyes.

Mel remained unruffled. "Crazy? Or did you use the old softball bat we found on your property?" She showed him the photo.

Newman sputtered, at a loss.

Sensing victory, Mel withdrew the crime scene images. Newman recoiled, any fight left draining away.

"We matched sand from the wildlife lot to residue on Foster's skull," Mel revealed. "It's over, Newman"

Collapsing forward, sobs wracked Newman's hulking frame. "Alright, it was me! I just snapped, I swear!"

As he confessed between gasps, Shane elicited the full story: ambushing Foster at the wildlife area, beating him with the bat, hastily disposing of the body in a random car trunk, moving Foster's car to his home, and burning Foster's wallet to cover his tracks.

With Newman processed for murder, Mel returned home, recounting the resolution to Dana on their porch as dusk settled over the village. She allowed herself to bask in the satisfaction of justice served for Greg Foster and his loved ones.

"I'm so proud of you for never giving up," Dana said, admiration in her tone.

"All in a day's work," Mel deflected, though she couldn't suppress a grin.

"Take the credit, babe. You earned it." Dana nudged her playfully.

Laughing, Mel clinked their sweet tea glasses together. "Maybe I did outdo myself this time," she conceded cockily.

They sat in contented silence as fireflies lit up around the darkening village. Mel felt peace blanket her, knowing this case that had plagued her was finally and conclusively solved.

***

Lance stood in the police impound lot, shifting his weight from foot to foot as he waited for the officer to bring out his prized vintage Cutlass Supreme. The bright sun glinted off the chain-link fence surrounding the rows of vehicles, but Lance barely noticed the glare. His mind was focused on the muscle car he hadn't seen in over a decade.

The sound of an engine rumbled to life, and Lance watched as an officer drove the gleaming blue Cutlass up to the gate. Lance's breath caught in his throat - even after all these years, she was still a beauty.

"Here she is, good as new," the officer said as he stepped out and handed Lance the keys. "We released the car back to you now that the investigation is completed."

Lance nodded, accepting the keys with trembling fingers. He slowly approached the driver's side, grasping the door handle but hesitating before getting in.

This car represented so many memories from his youth - cruising with friends, dates with his high school girlfriend, road trips. But now, its history was forever tainted by the grisly murder that happened just as they had been brought back together.

Lance vividly remembered the shock of seeing a body in the trunk after finally locating his stolen vehicle. He had learned not to ask too many questions from his sister-in-law, Sheriff Crane, but it still haunted him.

Taking a deep breath, Lance finally slid into the driver's seat. He caressed the glossy wooden steering wheel, emblazoned with the Oldsmobile logo. The buttery leather interior still smelled faintly of cherry air freshener, just as he recalled.

Turning the key in the ignition, the engine rumbled to life with a throaty purr. As Lance gripped the wheel, memories flooded back - so much nostalgia and yet so much pain now tied to this Cutlass.

Could he ever drive it again without picturing that gruesome discovery in the trunk? Or reliving the trauma of nearly being accused of murder himself? The car now carried a darkness that could never be outrun.

With a heavy sigh, Lance turned off the engine once more. He wasn't sure if keeping her was worth enduring the painful memories and lingering unease. For now, he would let his vintage Cutlass Supreme remain in uncertain limbo - like his feelings about reclaiming a past now stained by death.

CHAPTER 21

Mel stood at the front of the roll call and briefing room, her broad shoulders squared, and her gaze fixed ahead. Her hands clasped together in front of her, knuckles white with tension. She took a deep breath, steeling herself for the tough decision she was about to share.

"I know this news may come as a shock," Mel began, her voice steady despite the turmoil raging inside her. "But I've made a decision about my future here at the department."

Her eyes flickered over the faces of her colleagues, searching for any sign of dissent or disapproval. But all she saw were expressions of concern and curiosity, mixed with a healthy dose of respect.

"Over the past few months, I've been struggling with balancing my personal life and my duties as sheriff. It's not a simple task, as I'm sure many of you can understand."

Mel paused, taking another deep breath and gathering her thoughts.

"Ultimately, I've come to the difficult decision that it's time for me to step down as Sheriff of Muskingum County."

The room erupted into a chorus of murmurs and gasps, but Mel held up a hand to silence them.

"Please, let me finish," she said firmly. "I'm not leaving the department entirely. I'll be staying on for a little while in an advisory capacity. Sergeant Gates has agreed to step into the position of acting sheriff, and I have every confidence in his abilities to take over the department long term, should he choose to stand for election."

Mel turned to face Gates, who was sitting near the back of the room, his eyes fixed on her. "SGT Gates has been a valuable member of this department for many years, and I know he'll lead us with integrity and dedication."

There was a smattering of applause from the crowd, and Mel saw Gates nodding his agreement from his spot near the back of the room.

"I know this is a big change, but I have faith in every one of you. We will work together to ensure a smooth transition and to continue serving the people of Muskingum County with the same professionalism and commitment we always have."

"I want to express my gratitude for your support and dedication throughout my tenure as sheriff. It has been an honor to serve alongside all of you." Mel paused, taking a moment to look at each member of her team. They were her family, the people she had worked with day in and day out for years. It was hard to imagine leaving them behind. "I'll always be grateful for the friendships and memories I've made here."

She stepped away from the podium, feeling a weight lifted off her shoulders. As she made her way towards Gates, he stood up.

"Thank you for your service, Mel," he said, extending his hand. "I will make sure that your legacy lives on in this department."

Mel shook his hand, his grip firm and reassuring. A sense of relief flooded through her. She knew that the department was in good hands with Gates, and that she could now focus on her own priorities without the weight of the Sheriff's office hanging over her. Mel smiled, feeling a sense of hope and new beginnings. This wasn't the end of her journey - far from it - but it was a necessary step towards creating a better work-life balance and prioritizing the people she loved.

As other members of the department looked on, there were nods of approval and murmurs of agreement. They were all aware of the tremendous responsibility that came with being Sheriff, but they also knew that Gates was up for the challenge.

Mel stepped out of the conference room and made her way down the hallway, the sound of her footsteps echoing off the walls. She felt a sense of lightness in her step now that the weight of the Sheriff's office was no longer hanging over her.

As she walked, her mind wandered to thoughts of her family. She thought about her father, who had been struggling to keep up with his farm lately. The heart surgery had given him fresh energy, but it wasn't a cure all. With her new free time, she could finally spend more time helping him out. It would be good for both of them - a chance to reconnect after all these years.

CHAPTER 22

A Couple Weeks Later
Morelville, Ohio

Mel sat alone at the kitchen table, staring off into space. Her mind was racing with thoughts of the future and what lay ahead. Her decision filled her with a mix of excitement and uncertainty.

As she sat lost in thought, the sound of the front door opening pulled her back to reality. Andrea walked in with a smile, clearly excited to see Mel. "Hey there, stranger," Andrea said, walking over to give Mel a hug.

"Hey," Mel replied, returning the embrace before gesturing for Andrea to take a seat at the table. "Thanks for coming over."

"Of course, I wouldn't miss it," Andrea said, taking a seat across from Mel. "So, how's everything going? How are you feeling about your decision?"

Mel took a deep breath before responding. "Honestly, it's a mix of emotions. I'm excited to start this new chapter of my life, but I'm nervous about what the future holds. Being the sheriff has been such a big part of my identity for so long."

Andrea nodded in understanding. "I can imagine. But I know you'll figure it out. You always do."

"Thanks, Andrea," Mel said, smiling at the encouragement. She gestured to the coffeemaker. "A cup?"

"Yes, please, and thank you."

As Mel poured, she asked her friend, "So, how was your trip to Tennessee?"

Andrea's face lit up as she launched into an animated account of her adventures with Renee to Mel and Dana's cabin in the Smoky Mountains. As she spoke, Mel couldn't help but feel a sense of envy. It had been so long since she had been able to truly relax and enjoy herself without chaos surrounding her.

"Sounds like you had an amazing time," Mel said, feeling a twinge of regret that she and Dana hadn't been able to join them.

"We did," Andrea said, beaming. "It was just what we needed. And speaking of that, have you and Dana thought about taking a vacation soon? A real vacation?"

Mel shook her head. "Not really. With everything going on, it's hard to justify taking time off."

"Believe me, I understand," Andrea said, nodding sympathetically. "But it's important to take care of yourself too, Mel. You can't keep running at full speed forever. You've traded the craziness of the Sheriff's Department for the craziness of running the family farm."

"And all the crazy family that comes with it," Mel added. She knew Andrea was right, but the idea of stepping back even further from her responsibilities made her uneasy. She was used to being in control, and the thought of letting go was daunting. "Maybe you're right," she said, finally conceding. "We'll have to see what we can do."

"Good," Andrea said, smiling warmly. "Now, tell me more about this Gates guy who's taking your place."

Mel chuckled. "SGT Gates is a good man. He'll do a great job."

"He's got some big shoes to fill."

"He'll be fine. I'm not completely out of the picture. Not yet. I'll make sure he knows everything he needs to know to do the job...and what he has to do to work with you."

"What's that supposed to mean?" Andrea set down the coffee she'd been sipping and tried to look indignant but, she started laughing.

As the conversation continued, Mel couldn't help but feel a sense of gratitude for Andrea's unwavering support. It was moments like these that reminded her why their friendship meant so much to her.

***

Mel stood at the edge of the clear, bubbling stream that wound its way through her father's property. Jesse sat beside her on a weathered wooden bench, his line already cast into the water.

"Beautiful day," Jesse said, his voice gruff but warm.

"Sure is," Mel said, smiling. "Not too hot, not too cold. Just right for fishing."

"Yep," Jesse said, his eyes scanning the water. "Quiet too. Ain't nobody else around."

"Good," Mel said, feeling a sense of peace settle over her. "Just what we need."

They sat in companionable silence for a few minutes, the only sounds the gentle gurgling of the stream and the occasional chirp of a bird. Mel felt her thoughts drift to the future, to the changes that were coming with her decision to step down as sheriff.

"Been thinking a lot lately," she said, her voice low. "About what comes next, you know?"

"I do," Jesse said, turning to look at her. "What's on your mind?"

"Just...everything," Mel said, feeling a lump form in her throat. "I'm excited to have more time with Dana and the kids–Beth, Cole, Jef–to travel more, even take up some hobbies or something. But I'm also scared, you know? Scared about what it'll be like to not be sheriff anymore."

"Change is always scary," Jesse said, his hand resting gently on her arm. "But sometimes it's necessary. And from where I'm sitting, I'd say you've earned yourself a break."

"Thanks, Dad," Mel said, feeling a sense of gratitude wash over her. "I just want to make sure I'm doing the right thing, you know? For me, for my family, for the department."

"Of course," Jesse said, nodding. "But don't forget to think about yourself, too. You've been working hard for a long time, Mel. It's okay to take a step back and focus on what makes you happy."

Mel nodded, taking a deep breath of the fresh air. For a few moments, they both sat in silence, lost in their own thoughts.

"Speaking of happiness," Mel said, breaking the quiet. "What are your wishes for the farm, Dad? I want to make sure I'm doing right by you, too."

Jesse smiled, a twinkle in his eye. "Well now, that's a conversation we can have over some cold beers tonight if you're up for it."

"Sounds perfect," Mel said, grinning. As she watched, her father cast his line once more. She felt a sense of contentment settle over her. Whatever the future held, she knew she had her family by her side. And that was all that mattered.

Later that evening, Mel and her dad sat on the farmhouse porch, watching the sun set over the rolling hills. Mel cracked open a cold beer and handed one to her father.

"Thanks, hon," he said with a grin.

"Of course, Dad," Mel replied, taking a sip of her own drink. "I'm just glad we could spend some time together."

"Me too," Jesse said, his eyes crinkling at the corners. "Now, tell me more about this decision you've made."

Mel took a deep breath. She had been keeping quiet about stepping down for a few weeks, but it still felt scary to say she had gone ahead and done it out loud.

"I've stepped down as sheriff," she said, watching her father's face closely.

Jesse's expression didn't change, but Mel could sense his surprise.

"Really?" he said, nodding slowly. "Well, I'll be darned. That's big news, Mel. You talked about it in Tennessee. but we never got to finish that conversation."

Mel nodded. "Yeah. I know. It wasn't an easy decision for me, but I think it's the right one."

"Of course it is," Jesse said, putting a hand on Mel's shoulder. "You've done a heck of a job as Sheriff, Mel. You've made this county a safer place, and you've made your old man proud."

Mel felt a lump form in her throat. She knew how hard she had worked over the years, but to hear her father say it out loud meant everything to her.

"Thanks, Dad," she said, her voice catching slightly. "That means a lot to me."

"Anytime," Jesse said, squeezing her shoulder. "And just so you know, whatever you decide to do next, I'll be behind you 100%. You're my daughter, and I want you to be happy."

"Thanks, Dad," Mel said, feeling a sense of relief wash over her. For so long, she had been focused on her career, but now, with the support of her family, she could let herself imagine a different future. One where she had more time for the things that truly mattered.

As they sat in companionable silence, watching the stars twinkle in the night sky, Mel felt a sense of contentment settle over her. She had made the right choice, and she had the love and support of her family to help her navigate whatever came next. The conversation about the farm could wait another day.

AFTERWARD

L ate 2019...where to begin?

To make a very long story short, my wife and I got a foster care license in early October 2019, intending to take in a baby who was related to a family member by marriage. Two months before the baby was born, literally a week after we got our license, two foster children were placed with us, an eight-year-old boy and his four-year-old half-sister for a two-week respite/trial run with us as first-time foster parents.

I published Book 12 in the Morelville Mysteries series in November 2019. Life was good! The kids were still with us and a dream to have; the book did well, and readers loved the sneak peek at the case that would start off book 13...this book. I started working diligently on book 13, laying out the entire plot. I wrote a few chapters and, based on those, I planned an early spring 2020 release. Then, I loosely plotted books 14 through 16.

The story of the long-lost cutlass supreme is based on a true story, minus the body in the trunk. I've detailed that story in other places, including at the end of book 12. It was such a unique story; it really lit a fire under me to write about it when I first heard it.

Back in the land of reality, those two children were still here in December 2019 when the baby was born. We brought her home from the hospital when she was two days old with a Kinship Care agreement rather than as a foster child...another long story.

Time stood still for a couple of weeks as we, my wife in her 40s and I in my 50s, adjusted to life with a newborn and two additional children who were leaving their honeymoon period with us and showing all the signs of children affected by multiple traumas as so many foster children are.

The baby got RSV at two weeks old; a respiratory virus that affects children under two and the elderly. She would spend nine days in late December 2019 and early January 2020 fighting for every breath at Nationwide Children's Hospital. This book was laid aside as we fought alongside her and dealt with other issues at home, especially with one of the older children.

By late January 2020, some sanity had returned to our home. By late February, the baby was sleeping in longer stints at night without us worrying and fretting all night that she might stop breathing again. We thought things were looking up. They weren't. I thought I might take up this book again. I didn't.

The baby had major developmental problems. One of our foster children had major problems of another kind. And then there was Covid...

By May, pre-school closed for the four-year-old, school went online for the eight-year-old, and my wife was sent home to work. Having everyone home all day, every day, would drag out for the next few months. The strains of trying to care for a special needs infant while homeschooling a preschooler and a fourth grader, one of them with deep-seated issues, and trying to maintain an environment that was productive for my wife's work as well Wore. Me. Out.

I admit, I gave up on this book. In fact, I wrote barely a word of anything for several months. 2020 was a wash for me like it was for so many other authors.

I've put out several short stories since the end of 2020. I've written a few novellas/shorter novels. Some of the short stories had mystery and suspense elements, but the longer works I've published are all romance. I was reluctant to pick this series back up after being away from it for so long.

No longer. I went back early in the spring and re-read 'Tennessee Bound' myself. I looked over my old outline and tweaked it a bit. Once grounded again, I started writing with a rewrite of the first couple of chapters and I let the rest flow.

I know long-term fans of this series have been waiting a few years now for this book. And, if they've read this far, they're probably not happy about the direction things are heading. For them I say this; beyond this book, three more books are planned. I'm still in love with the basic outlines I did for books 14, 15, and 16 and they will be written. I make no promises beyond Book 16, but I promise you'll be surprised at some twists in the road ahead for Sheriff Mel and family.

Oh, and the kids? They're still here. The first two are eight and thirteen now. We adopted them in July of this year (2023). In 2021, we had another placement, a then two-year-old boy. He's still with us too and is now four. He and the three-year-old 'baby' will be adopted in December, giving 'us' four kids and me five. I have a biological son in his late twenties. Yes, to answer the obvious question, it's crazy hard to do this all again at my age, but I wouldn't change it for the world.

~Anne

ABOUT THE AUTHOR

Anne Hagan is the author of over twenty full-length works of fiction in the mystery, romance, and thriller genres. She writes of family, friends, love, murder, and mayhem in no particular order and often all in the same story. She's a half owner of the weekly discount eBook newsletter, MyLesfic, a wife, parent, foster parent, and an Army veteran. When she writes, she draws from her experiences because truth is often stranger than fiction.

Connect with Anne

For the latest information about upcoming releases, other projects, sample chapters and everything personal, check out Anne's site at https://AnneHaganAuthor.com/ or like Anne on Facebook at https://www.facebook.com/AuthorAnneHagan. You can also connect with Anne on Twitter @AuthorAnneHagan.

Join Anne's Email List

Are you interested in free books? How about free short stories? For those and all the latest news on new releases, opportunities to get review copies of all of her new releases and more, please consider joining Anne's email list at: https://www.AnneHaganAuthor.com by filling in the pop up or using the brief form in the sidebar.

ALSO BY

The books of the Morelville Mysteries series Anne's sapphic themed mystery/romance series:

Relic: The Morelville Mysteries–Book 1–The first Dana and Sheriff Mel mystery and the first book in the Morelville saga.
Cases collide for two star crossed ladies of law enforcement!

Busy Bees: The Morelville Mysteries–Book 2
Romance and Murder Mix in the Latest Story Featuring Sheriff Mel Crane and Special Agent Dana Rossi!

Dana's Dilemma: The Morelville Mysteries–Book 3–The relationship matures between Mel and Dana in an installment that features a breaking Amish character, an ex-girlfriend, a conniving politician, and murder.

Elections and Old Loves Combine with Deadly Results in a Romantic Mystery Featuring Sheriff Mel Crane and Special Agent Dana Rossi!

Hitched and Tied: The Morelville Mysteries–Book 4
Mel and Dana attempt to bring their growing romantic relationship full circle, but family, duty, and family duties all conspire to get in the way.

Viva Mama Rossi!: The Morelville Mysteries–Book 5–The 5th tale in the Morelville Mysteries and the book that gives fans a full introduction to future Morelville Cozies series sleuths Faye Crane (Mel's mom) and Chloe Rossi (Dana's Mama). The two series stand-alone, but they're certainly better together.
A delayed honeymoon getaway takes a deadly turn for newlyweds Mel and Dana; meanwhile, two meddling mothers won't let sleeping fisherman lie in the latest Morelville Mystery.

A Crane Christmas: The Morelville Mysteries–Book 6
Is it the Christmas season or the 'silly season'?

Mad for Mel: The Morelville Mysteries–Book 7
Rival gangs will stop at nothing to gain sole control of the drug trade in Muskingum County, and they've picked Valentine's week to create a firestorm of murder and mayhem as they battle each other for supremacy.

Hannah's Hope: The Morelville Mysteries–Book 8
A young mother with a troubled past seeks help from Mel and Dana,
but is their effort to assist her too little, too late?

The Turkey Tussle: The Morelville Mysteries–Book 9
The old-fashioned country village of Morelville holds a secret.

Sullied Sally: The Morelville Mysteries–Book 10
An unsolved murder, over 40 years in the past, leads to the discovery
of a new victim and the return of an old stalker.

Finding Sheila: The Morelville Mysteries–Book 11
A woman, imprisoned for manslaughter, disappears without a trace
during transport between states, and it's all up to Dana to find her.

Tennessee Bound: The Morelville Mysteries–Book 12
The politics and the paper-pushing are wearing on Sheriff Mel. Will
she chuck it all?

Cutlass Cadaver: The Morelville Mysteries – Book 13
Sheriff Mel Crane faces dual mysteries threatening her family and her
career.

***

A spinoff of Anne's Morelville Mysteries series, The Morelville Cozies series features meddling mother sleuths Faye Crane and Chloe Rossi getting mixed up in mysteries all their own.

The Passed Prop: The Morelville Cozies–Book 1
Chloe Rossi wants to retire with her husband and move away from suburban sprawl to bucolic Morelville; the only trouble is, Morelville is experiencing its worst crime wave ever, and Marco Rossi wants no part of a move there. What to do?

Opera House Ops: The Morelville Cozies–Book 2
Murder and other sinister goings-on at a vacant 1800s era opera house in Morelville and a modern-day property developer who wants to raze the historic building for his own gain have the village residents all tied up in knots and Faye Crane trying to play savior to history.

The Conjuring Commedienne: The Morelville Cozies–Book 3
Faye thinks Hattie's a suspect. Chloe thinks she's a kindred soul. Only Hattie knows for sure!

***

Anne's Romance Novels and Novellas:

Fake Marriage Planning Inc
We don't supply the fiancee!

Misfit Christmas – A Colorado Holiday Romance

Broken Women
Can two women, unlucky in love, find solace in each other?

Healing Embrace–The stand-alone sequel to Broken Women
Barb and Janet were a couple... and then they weren't. What now?

Steamboat Reunion–the third and final book in the Barb and Janet
series
Can you go home again?

A Sweetwater Christmas
Traditional and progressive meet in ruby red west-central Texas...
This novella is a significant expansion of the short story, Loving Blue
in Red States: Sweetwater Texas.

Christmas Cakes and Kisses
Two different worlds brought together by cake...

***

Steel City Confidential–Anne's first legal thriller (AKA The Thelma and Louise Book)
Clients hide things from their lawyers all the time. Pam Wilson makes it an art form.

***

Published Short Stories

Series and Collections:

Loving Blue in Red States
A sapphic romance *short story* series that kicks off with a visit to the little town of Sweetwater, Texas. It's followed by stops in Birmingham, Alabama, Jackson Hole, Wyoming, Perryville, Missouri, Salt Lake City, Utah, Savannah, Georgia, Wall, South Dakota and East

Tennessee. There's also an international contribution to the series,
Kilbirnie Scotland authored by Kitty McIntosh.

Sapphic Sweets Romantic short stories – Some sweet. Some with a
little heat.

Individual Short Stories:

A Con Con – Mystery/Suspense

Before Dana – Erotica/Erotic Romance featuring Mel from the
Morelville Mysteries Series

Crevice Chaos – Suspense/Thriller

Hazard Pay – Mystery/Suspense

Hunting You Down – Suspense

Midnight Slain in Georgia – Paranormal/Suspense/Thriller – features
two characters from the Loving Blue in Red States short story, Savannah Georgia

Secret Masquerade – Erotic Suspense featuring Sheriff Mel from the
Morelville Mysteries Series

Sundae Fun Day – Sweet romance

Treasure Hunted – Mystery – A Mel and Dana Short

<u>Waiting for You</u> - Romance

www.ingramcontent.com/pod-product-compliance
Lightning Source LLC
Chambersburg PA
CBHW061154170626
46809CB00003B/1095